CHRISTMAS BABY
FOR THE GREEK

CHRISTMAS BABY FOR THE GREEK

JENNIE LUCAS

MILLS & BOON

First published in Great Britain 2019
by Mills & Boon, an imprint of HarperCollins*Publishers*
1 London Bridge Street, London, SE1 9GF

Large Print edition 2020

© 2019 Jennie Lucas

ISBN: 978-0-263-08425-2

MIX
Paper from
responsible sources
FSC
www.fsc.org
FSC C007454

This book is produced from independently certified FSC™ paper to ensure responsible forest management. For more information visit www.harpercollins.co.uk/green.

Printed and bound in Great Britain
by CPI Group (UK) Ltd, Croydon, CR0 4YY

CHAPTER ONE

WAS THERE ANYTHING worse than a wedding on Christmas Eve, with glittering lights sparkling against the snow, holly and ivy decking the halls and the scent of winter roses in the air?

If there was, Holly Marlowe couldn't think of it.

"You may now kiss the bride," the minister said, beaming between the newly married couple.

Heartbroken, Holly watched as Oliver—the boss she'd loved in devoted silence for three years—beamed back and lowered his head to kiss the bride.

Her younger sister, Nicole.

The guests in the pews looked enchanted at the couple's passionate embrace, but Holly felt sick. Fidgeting in her tight red maid-of-honor dress, she looked up at the grand stained-glass windows, then back at the nave of the old New York City church, lavishly decorated with flickering white candles and red roses.

Finally, the newly married couple pulled apart from the kiss. Snatching her bouquet back from Holly's numb fingers, the bride lifted her new husband's hand triumphantly in the air.

"Best Christmas ever!" Nicole cried.

There was a wave of adoring laughter and applause. And though Holly had always loved Christmas, striving to make it magical and full of treats each year for her little sister since their parents had died, she thought she'd hate it for the rest of her life.

No. A lump rose in Holly's throat. She couldn't think that way. She couldn't be selfish. Nicole and Oliver were in love. She should be happy for them. She forced herself to smile as the "Hallelujah" Chorus pounded from the organ in the alcove above.

Smiling, the bride and groom started back down the aisle. And Holly suddenly faced the best man. Oliver's cousin, and his boss. Which made him her boss's boss.

Stavros Minos.

Dark, tall and broad-shouldered, the powerful Greek billionaire seemed out of place in the old stone church. The very air seemed to vibrate back from him, moving to give him space. *He* hadn't been forced to wear some ridiculous outfit that made him look like a deranged Christmas lounge singer. Of course not. She looked over his sleek suit enviously. She couldn't imagine anyone forcing Stavros Minos to do anything.

Then Holly looked up, and the Greek's black eyes cut through her soul.

He glanced with sardonic amusement between her and the happy couple, as they continued to walk down the aisle to the cheers of their guests. And his cruel, sensual lips curved up at the edges, as if he knew exactly how her heart had been broken.

Holly's mouth went dry. No. No, he couldn't. No one must ever know that she'd loved Oliver. Because he wasn't just her boss now. He was her sister's husband. She had to pretend it never happened.

The truth was nothing *had* happened. She'd never said a word about her feelings to anyone, especially Oliver. The man had no idea that while working as his secretary, Holly had been secretly consumed by pathetic, unrequited love. No one had any idea. No one, it seemed, except Stavros Minos.

But it shouldn't surprise her the billionaire Greek playboy might see things no other person could. Nearly twenty years ago, as a teenager, he'd single-handedly started a tech company that now owned half the world. He was often in the news, both for his high-powered business dealings and conquests of the world's most beautiful women. Now, as organ music thundered relentlessly around them, Stavros looked at Holly with a strange knowing in his eyes.

Wordlessly, he held out his arm.

Reluctantly, Holly took it, and tried not to notice how muscled his arm was beneath his sleek black jacket. His biceps had to be bigger than her thigh! It seemed ridiculously unfair that a man so rich and powerful could also be so good-looking. It was why she'd carefully avoided looking at him whenever she'd liaised with his executive assistants—he had three of them—at work.

Shivering, she avoided looking at him again now as they followed Oliver and Nicole. The faces of the guests slid by as Holly smiled blindly at everyone in the packed wooden pews until she thought her face might crack.

Outside the old stone church, on a charming, historical lane in the Financial District, more guests waited to cheer for the couple, tossing red and white rose petals that fell against the thin blanket of snow on the ground.

The afternoon sunlight was weak and gray

against the lowering clouds when Holly reached the safety of the waiting limo. Dropping Stavros's arm, she scrambled inside and turned to stare fiercely out the window, blinking fast so no one would see her tears.

She couldn't be sad. Not today. Not ever. She was happy for her sister and Oliver, happy they'd be leaving her today to start new adventures together around the world. *Happy.*

"Whew." Nicole flopped into the seat across from her in a wave of white tulle that took most of the space in the back of the limo. She grinned at her new husband beside her. "We did it! We're married!"

"Finally," Oliver drawled, all lazy charm as he looked down at his bride. "That was a lot of work. But then, I never thought I'd let anyone put the marriage noose round my neck."

"'Til you met me," Nicole murmured, turning her face up to be kissed.

Smiling, he lowered his head. "Exactly."

Holly felt her own seat move as Stavros Minos sat beside her. As the door closed behind him, and the limo pulled away from the curb, she unwillingly breathed in his intoxicating scent of musk and power.

Oliver turned smugly to his cousin. "How

about it, Stavros? Did the ceremony give you any ideas?"

The Greek tycoon's handsome face was colder than the icy winter air outside. "Such as you can't imagine."

How dare he be so rude? Holly thought incredulously. But then, the commitment-phobic playboy famously despised weddings. He obviously was unhappy to be forced to attend his cousin's wedding. And unlike Holly, he didn't feel any compunction to hide his feelings. Luckily, the happy couple didn't seem to notice.

Oliver snorted. "I was going to invite Uncle Aristides today, him being family and all that, but I knew you wouldn't like it."

"Generous of you." His voice was flat.

Holly envied Stavros Minos's coldness right now, when she herself felt heartbroken and raw. Her sister's pressure for Holly to move with them to Hong Kong after they returned from their honeymoon in Aruba had been ratcheted up to an explosive level. Oliver had already quit at Minos International. If Holly stayed, she'd soon be working for the notoriously unpleasant VP of Operations. Or else she had a standing offer from a previous employer who'd moved back to Europe.

But if she was going to leave New York, shouldn't she move to Hong Kong, and work for Oliver in his new job? Shouldn't she devote herself to her baby sister's happiness, forever and ever?

"You really hate weddings, don't you, Stavros?" Oliver grinned at his cousin. "At least I won't have to see your grouchy face at the office anymore, old man. Your loss is Sinistech's gain."

"Right." Stavros shrugged. "Let another company deal with your three-hour martini lunches."

"Quite." Oliver's grin widened, then he licked his lips. "I can hardly wait to explore Hong Kong's delights."

"Me, too," Nicole said.

Oliver nearly jumped, as if he'd forgotten his bride beside him. "Naturally." He suddenly looked at Holly. "Did Nicole convince you yet? Will you come and work as my secretary there?"

Feeling everyone's eyes on her, her cheeks went red-hot. She stammered, "D-don't be silly."

"You mustn't be selfish," Oliver insisted. "I can't cope without you. Who else can keep me organized in my new job?"

"And I might get pregnant soon," Nicole said anxiously. "Who will take care of the baby if you're not around?"

The ache in Holly's throat sharpened to a razor blade. Watching her sister marry the man she loved and then leave for the other side of the world was hard enough. But the suggestion that Holly should live with them and raise their children was pure cruelty.

As of her birthday yesterday, she was a twenty-seven-year-old virgin. She was a secretary, a sister, and perhaps soon, an aunt. But would she ever be more? A wife? A mother?

Would she ever meet a man she could love, who would love her in return? Would she ever be the most important person in the world to anyone?

At twenty-seven, it was starting to seem unlikely. She'd spent nearly a decade raising her sister since their parents died. She'd spent the last three years taking care of Oliver at work. Maybe that was all she was meant to do. Take care of Nicole and Oliver, watch them love each other and raise their children. Maybe Holly was meant only to be support staff in life. Never the star. The thought caused a stab of pain through her heart.

She choked out, "You'll be fine without me."

"Fine!" Indignantly, Nicole shook her head.

"It would be a disaster! You have to come with us to Hong Kong, Holly. *Please!*"

Her sister spoke with the same wheedling tone she'd used since she was a child to get her own way. The same one she'd used four weeks ago to convince Holly to arrange her sudden wedding— using the same Christmas details that Holly had once dreamed of for her own wedding someday.

Until she'd realized there was no point in saving all her own Christmas wedding dreams for a marriage that would never happen. If any man was ever going to be interested in her, it would have happened by now. And it hadn't. Her sister was the one with the talent in that arena. Blonde, tiny and beautiful, Nicole had always had a strange power over men, and at twenty-two, she'd learned how to use it well.

But even Holly had never imagined, when she'd introduced her to Oliver last summer at a company picnic, that it would end like this.

Looking at her sister, Holly suddenly noticed Nicole's bare neck. "Where's Mom's gold-star necklace, Nicole?"

Touching her bare collarbone above her neckline, her sister ducked her head. "It's somewhere in all the boxes. I'm sure I'll find it when I unpack in Hong Kong."

"You lost Mom's necklace?" Holly felt stricken. It was bad enough their parents hadn't lived to see their youngest daughter get married, but if Nicole had lost the precious gold-star necklace their mother had always worn…

"I didn't lose it," Nicole said irritably. She shrugged. "It's somewhere."

"And don't try to change the subject, Holly," Oliver said sharply. "You're being stubborn and selfish to stay in New York, when I need you so badly."

Selfish. The accusation hit Holly like a blow. Was she being selfish to stay, when they needed her? Selfish to still hope she could find her own happiness, instead of putting their needs first forever?

"I… I'm not trying to be," she whispered. As the limo drove north toward Midtown, Holly looked out the window, toward the bright Christmas lights and colorful window displays as the limo passed the department stores on Sixth Avenue. The sidewalks were filled with shoppers carrying festive bags and wrapped packages, rushing to buy gifts to put under the Christmas tree and fill stockings tomorrow morning. She saw happy children wearing Santa hats and beaming smiles.

A memory went through her of Nicole at that age, her smiling, happy face missing two front teeth as she'd hugged Holly tight and cried, "I wuv you, Howwy!"

A lump rose in Holly's throat. Nicole was her only family. If her baby sister truly needed her, maybe she *was* being selfish, thinking of her own happiness. Maybe she should just—

"Let me get this straight." Stavros Minos's voice was acidic as he suddenly leaned forward. "You want Miss Marlowe to quit her job at Minos International and move to Hong Kong? To do your office work for you, Oliver, all day, then take care of your children all night?"

Oliver scowled. "It's none of your business, Stavros."

"Your concern does you credit, Mr. Minos," Nicole interceded, giving him a charming smile, "but taking care of people is what Holly does best. She's taken care of me since I was twelve. I can't imagine her ever wanting to stop taking care of me."

"Of us," Oliver said.

Stavros lifted his sensual lips into a smile that showed the white glint of his teeth as he turned to Holly. "Is that true?"

He was looking at her so strangely. She stammered, "A-anyone would feel the same."

"I wouldn't."

"Of course you wouldn't," Oliver said with a snort, leaning back in the seat. "Minos men are selfish to the bone. We do what we like, and everyone else be damned."

"What is that supposed to mean?" his wife said.

He winked. "It's part of our charm, darling."

But Nicole didn't seem terribly charmed. With a flare of her nostrils, she turned to Holly. "I can't just leave you in New York. You wouldn't know what to do with yourself. You'd be so alone."

She stiffened. "I have friends…"

"But not family," she said impatiently. "And it's not very likely you ever will, is it?"

"Will what?"

"Have a husband or children of your own. I mean, come on." She gave a good-natured snort. "You've never even had a serious boyfriend. Do you really want to die alone?"

Holly stared at her sister in the back of the limo.

Nicole was right. And tomorrow, for the first time in her life, Holly would spend Christmas Day alone.

Christmas, and the rest of her life.

Her eyes met Stavros's in the back of the limo. His handsome features looked as hard and cold as a marble statue, his black eyes icy as a mid-winter's night. Then his expression suddenly changed.

"I'm afraid Miss Marlowe can't possibly go to Hong Kong," he said. "Because I need another executive assistant. So I'm giving her a promotion."

"What?" gasped Oliver.

"What?" gasped Nicole.

Holly looked at him sharply, blinking back tears. "What?"

His expression gentled. "Will you come work directly for me, Miss Marlowe? It will mean long hours, but a sizable raise. I'll double your salary."

"But—" Swallowing, Holly whispered, "Why me?"

"Because you're the best." His jaw, dark with five-o'clock shadow, tightened. "And because I can."

Stavros hadn't meant to get involved. Oliver was right. This was none of his business.

He didn't care about his cousin. Cousin or not,

the man was a useless bastard. Stavros regretted the day he'd hired him. Oliver had done a poor job as VP of Marketing. He'd been within a day of being fired when he'd taken the "surprise offer" from Hong Kong. Stavros was glad to see him go. He suspected Oliver might be surprised when his new employers actually expected him to work for his salary.

Stavros didn't much care for his cousin's new bride, either. In spite of his own turmoil last night, he'd actually tried to warn Nicole about Oliver's cheating ways at the rehearsal dinner. But the blonde had just cut him off. So she knew what she was getting into; she just didn't care.

He didn't give a damn about either of them.

But Holly Marlowe—she was different.

Stavros suspected it was only through the hardworking secretary's efforts that Oliver had managed to stay afloat these last three years. Holly worked long hours at the office then probably nights and weekends at home, doing Oliver's job for him. Everyone at the New York office loved kind, dependable Miss Marlowe, from the janitors to the COO. Tender-hearted, noble, self-sacrificing… Holly Marlowe was the most respected person in the New York office, Stavros included.

But she was totally oppressed by these two selfish people, who, instead of thanking her for all she'd done, seemed intent on taking her indentured servitude with them to Hong Kong.

Two days ago, Stavros might have shrugged it off. People had the right to make their own choices, even stupid ones.

But not after the news he'd received yesterday. Now, for the first time he was thinking about what his own legacy would be after he was gone. And it wasn't a pretty picture.

"You can't have Holly! I need her!" Oliver exploded. At Stavros's fierce glare, his cousin glanced uneasily at his wife. "*We* need her."

"You don't want some stupid promotion, do you, Holly?" Nicole wailed.

But Holly's face was shining as she looked at Stavros. "Do—do you mean it?"

"I never say anything I don't mean." As they drove north, past bundled-up tourists and sparkling lights and brightly decorated department-store windows, his gaze unwillingly traced over her pretty face and incredible figure. Until he'd stood across from her in the old stone church by candlelight, he'd never realized how truly beautiful Holly Marlowe was.

The truth was, he hadn't *wanted* to notice.

Beautiful women were a dime a dozen in his world, while truly competent, highly driven secretaries were few. And Holly had hidden her beauty, making herself nearly invisible at the office, yanking her fiery red hair in a matronly bun, never wearing makeup, working quietly behind the scenes in loose-cut beige skirt suits and sensible shoes.

Was this what she'd looked like all the time? Right under his nose?

Her bright, wide-set green eyes looked up at him, luminous beneath dramatic black lashes. Her skin was pale except for a smattering of freckles over her nose. Her lips were red and delectable as she nibbled them with white, even teeth. Her thick, curly red-gold hair spilled over her shoulders. And that tight red dress—

That dress—

Stavros obviously wasn't dead yet, because it set his pulse racing.

The bodice was low-cut, clinging to full, delicious breasts he'd never imagined existed beneath those baggy beige suits. As she moved, the knit fabric clung to her curves. He'd gotten a look at her deliciously full backside as they'd left the church, too.

All things he would have to ignore once she

worked for him. Deliberately, he looked away. He didn't seduce women who worked for him. Why would he, when beautiful women were so plentiful in his world, and truly spectacular employees more precious than diamonds?

Sex was an amusement, nothing more. But for years, his company had been his life.

And the reason Holly chose to dress so plainly in the office was obviously that she wanted to be valued for her accomplishments and hard work, not her appearance. In that, they were the same. From the time he was a child, Stavros had wanted to do important things. He'd wanted to change the world.

But that wasn't all they had in common. He'd seen her tortured expression as she'd looked at Oliver. So Stavros and Holly each had secrets they didn't want to talk about.

To anyone.

Ever.

But her inexplicable infatuation for Oliver couldn't possibly last. When she recovered from it, like someone healing from a bad cold, she'd realize she'd dodged a bullet.

As for Stavros's secret, people would figure it out for themselves when he dropped dead. Which, according to his doctor's prognosis, would happen in about six to nine months. He blinked.

All the life he'd left unlived...

Just a few days ago, Stavros had vaguely assumed he'd have another fifty years. Instead, he'd be unlikely to see his thirty-seventh birthday next September.

He would die alone, with no one but his lawyers and stockholders to mourn him. His company would be his only legacy. Estranged from his father, and feeling as he did about Oliver, Stavros would likely leave his shares to charity.

Poor Stavros, his ex-mistresses would say. Then they'd roll over and enjoy their hot new lovers in bed.

Poor Minos, his business associates would say. Then they'd focus on exciting new technology to buy and sell.

And he'd be dirt in the ground. Never once knowing what it felt like to commit to anything but work. Not even leaving a son or daughter to carry on his name.

Looking back, Stavros saw it all with painful clarity, now that his life was coming to an end. And he had only himself to blame. Nicole's thoughtlessly cruel words floated back to him. *Do you really want to die alone?*

Christmas lights sparkled on Sixth Avenue, as yellow taxis filled with people on the way to family dinners rushed past in the rapidly falling twilight. The limo turned east, finally pulling into the entrance of the grand hotel overlooking Central Park.

"This isn't over, Holly," Oliver said firmly. "I'm going to persuade you."

"You'll come with us," Nicole said, smiling as she smoothed back her veil.

The uniformed driver opened the back door of the limousine. Oliver got out first, then gallantly reached back to assist his glamorous bride. Nicole's white tulle skirts swirled in a train with her fluttery white veil, her diamond tiara sparkling. Tourists gaped at them on the sidewalk. A few lifted their phones for pictures, clearly believing they were seeing royalty. The new Mr. and Mrs. Oliver Minos waved at them regally as they swept into the grand hotel to take photos before the guests arrived for a ballroom reception.

Silence fell in the back of the limo. For a moment, Holly didn't move. Stavros looked at her.

"Don't give in to them, Holly," he urged in a low voice. It was the first time he'd used her first name. "Stick up for yourself. You're worth so much more than they are."

Her green eyes widened, then suddenly glistened with tears. She whispered, "How can you say that?"

"Because it's true," he said harshly. He got out of the limo and held out his hand for her.

Blinking fast, she slowly placed her hand in his.

And it happened.

Stavros had slept with many women, beautiful and famous and powerful, models and starlets and even a Nobel laureate.

But when he touched Holly's hand to help her from the limo, he felt something he'd never experienced before. An electric shock sizzled him to his core.

He looked down at her as he pulled her to the sidewalk, his heart pounding strangely as he helped her to her feet. Snowflakes suddenly began falling as she looked up, lingering in his arms.

Then Holly's gaze fell on the lacy white snowflakes. With a joyous laugh, she dropped his hand, looking up with wonder at the gray lowering sky.

Without her warmth, Stavros again felt the winter chill beneath his tuxedo jacket. The world became a darker place, freezing him, reminding him he'd soon feel nothing at all. He stood very still, watching her. Then he lifted his face to the sky, wondering if this would be the last time he'd feel snowflakes on his skin.

If only he could have at least left a child behind. He suddenly wanted that so badly it hurt. If only he could have left some memory of his existence on earth.

But the women he knew were as ambitious and heartless as he was. He couldn't leave an innocent child in their care. Children needed someone willing to put their needs above her own. He knew no woman like that. None at all.

Then he heard a laugh of pure delight, and Stavros looked down at Holly Marlowe's beautiful, shining, tenderhearted eyes.

"Can you believe it?" Stretching her arms wide, laughing like a child, she whirled in a circle, holding out her tongue to taste the snowflakes. She looked like an angel. Her eyes danced as she cried, "It's snowing at my sister's wedding! On Christmas Eve!"

And all of the busy avenue, the tourists, the horse-drawn carriages, the taxis blaring Christmas music, faded into the background. Stavros saw only her.

CHAPTER TWO

THE GRAND TWO-STORY hotel ballroom was a winter wonderland, filled with white-and-silver Christmas trees twinkling like stars. Each of the twenty big round tables had centerpieces of red roses, deep scarlet against the white. It was even more beautiful than Holly had dreamed. A lump rose in her throat as she slowly looked around her.

She'd imagined a wedding reception like this long ago, as a lonely nineteen-year-old, cutting out photographs from magazines and putting them in an idea book each night while her little sister slept in the dark apartment. Holly had been alone, her friends all in college or partying in clubs.

Holly didn't regret her choice to give up her college scholarship and come home. After their parents had died in the car accident on their anniversary, she'd known she couldn't leave Nicole to foster care. But sometimes, she'd felt so trapped, chained by the responsibilities of love. She'd felt so lonely, without a partner, and with a teenaged sister who'd often shouted at Holly in her own grief and frustrated rage.

So to comfort herself, Holly had created the dream book. It had kept her company, until Nicole had left for college three years ago, and Holly had started working for Oliver.

In her romantic fantasy of long ago, she'd always imagined she'd be the bride in the white princess dress, dancing with an adoring groom. Now, as she watched Nicole and Oliver dance their first dance as husband and wife, surrounded by all their adoring friends, she told herself she'd never been so happy.

"They really do make a perfect couple." Stavros's low, husky voice spoke beside her. Somehow, his tone made the words less than complimentary.

"Yes," Holly said, moving slightly to make sure they didn't accidentally touch. When he'd helped her from the limo earlier, her whole body had trembled. It was totally ridiculous. She was sure Stavros Minos hadn't felt anything. Why would he? While Holly, hours later, still felt burning hot, lit up from within, whenever the Greek billionaire drew close. Whenever he even looked at her. She had to get ahold of herself, if she was going to be his assistant!

What was wrong with her? Holly didn't understand. How could she feel so—so aware of Stavros, when she was in love with Oliver?

She was, wasn't she?

But she didn't want to love Oliver anymore. It had done nothing but hurt her. And now he was her brother-in-law, it felt slimy and wrong. She wanted to reach inside her soul and turn off her feelings like a light—

"You arranged the reception, too, didn't you?" Stavros said, looking at the Christmas fantasy around them.

She forced herself to smile. "I wanted my sister to have a dream wedding. I did my best."

Stavros abruptly turned to look at the happy couple, dancing now in front of the largest white-flocked tree, decorated with white lights and silver stars. He took a long drink of the amber-colored liquid he'd gotten from the open bar. "You are a good person."

Again, the words should have been a compliment, but they weren't. Not the way he said them. She tried to read his expression, but his darkly handsome face was inscrutable. She shook her head. "You must hate all this."

"This?"

"Being best man at a wedding." Holly shrugged. "You're the most famously commitment-phobic bachelor in the city."

He took another deliberate drink. "Let's just say love is something I've never had the good fortune to experience."

More irony, she thought. Then his black eyes burned through her, reminding her he knew about her secret love for Oliver. Her cheeks burned.

Looking toward the beautiful bride and handsome groom slow-dancing in the center of the ballroom, the very picture of fairy-tale love, she mumbled, "You're right. They do make a perfect couple."

"Stop it," he said sharply, as if he was personally annoyed.

"Stop what?"

"Take off the rose-colored glasses."

Her mouth dropped. "What?"

"You'd have to be stupid to love Oliver. And whatever you are, Miss Marlowe, you're not stupid."

The conversation had taken a strangely personal turn. Her heart pounded. But there seemed no point in trying to lie. She'd never dared to give voice to her feelings before. She whispered, "How did you guess?"

He rolled his eyes. "You wear your heart on your face." He paused. "I'm sure Oliver knows exactly how you feel."

Horror went through her. "Oh, no—he couldn't possibly—"

"Of course he knows," Stavros said brutally. "How else could he have taken advantage of you all these years?"

"Advantage?" Astonished, she looked up at him. "Of me?"

He looked down at her seriously. "I have ten thousand employees around the world. And from what everyone tells me, you're the hardest working one."

"Mr. Minos—"

"Call me Stavros," he ordered.

"Stavros." She blushed. "I'm sure that's not true. I go home at six every night—"

"Yes, home to do Oliver's paperwork. Never asking for a raise, even though you were paying for your sister to go to college. Which, by the way, she could have gotten a job and paid for herself."

Her blush deepened in confusion. "I take care of my sister because—because she's my responsibility. I take care of Oliver because, because," she continued, faltering, "I'm his employee. At least I was…"

"And because you're in love with him."

"Yes," she whispered, her heart in her throat.

"And now he's impulsively married your sister, and instead of being angry—" he motioned at the winter wonderland around them "—you arranged all this."

"Except for this dress." She looked down ruefully at the tight red dress, wishing she was dressed in that modest burgundy gown she'd selected. "Nicole picked it out. She said my dress was the frumpiest thing she'd ever seen and she wasn't going to let it ruin her wedding photographs."

"They really do deserve each other, don't they?" he murmured. Then he glanced down at her and growled, "You look beautiful in that dress."

Another compliment that didn't sound like a compliment. If anything, he sounded angry about it. His jaw was tight as he looked away.

Was he mocking her? She didn't understand why he would tell her she was beautiful but sound almost furious about it. Her cheeks burned as she muttered, "Thanks."

For a moment, the two of them stood apart from the crowd, watching as the bridal couple finished their dance with a long, flashy kiss. The guests applauded then went out to join them on the dance floor. Feeling awkward, Holly started to turn away.

Stavros stopped her, his dark eyes glittering as he said huskily, "Dance with me."

"What? No."

Broad-shouldered and powerful in his tuxedo, he towered over her like a dark shadow. Lifting a sardonic eyebrow, he just held out his hand, waiting.

What was he playing at? Stavros took starlets and models to his bed. Why would he be interested in dancing with a plain, ordinary girl like her? She looked up at him. His handsome face was arrogant, as untouchable and distant as a star.

"You don't have to feel sorry for me," she said stiffly.

"I don't."

"Or if you think it's a requirement, because you're best man and I'm maid of honor—"

"Do I strike you as a man who gives a damn about other people's rules?" he asked, cutting her off. "I just want you to see the truth."

"What's that?" Half-mesmerized, she let him pull her into his powerful arms. Electricity crackled up her arm as she felt the heat of his palm against hers. She looked up at his face. His jawline was dark with five-o'clock shadow below razor-sharp cheekbones. There was a strange darkness in his black eyes, a vibrating tension from his muscular body beneath the well-cut tuxedo.

"You don't love my cousin. You never did."

She tried to pull away. "You have some nerve to—"

Holding her hand implacably in his own, he led her out onto the dance floor, where guests swayed to the slow romantic Christmas music of the orchestra.

She felt everyone looking at her. The women, with a mix of envy and bewilderment, the men, with interest, their eyes lingering on her uncomfortably low neckline.

Even Nicole and Oliver paused to gape at the sight of Stavros leading her out on the dance floor. Holly felt equally bewildered. Stavros could dance with anyone. Why would he choose her? Had he lost some kind of bet?

Surely this couldn't just be to convince Holly she had no real feelings for Oliver.

But if he could, how wonderful would that be?

Suddenly, Holly wanted it more than anything in the world.

Stavros led her confidently to the center of the dance floor, forcing others to move aside to make way for them. Pulling her against his chest, he looked down at her. She felt his dark gaze burn through her body, all the way to her toes. He looked at her almost as if he—

Desired her?

No. Holly's cheeks went hot. That was a step too far. No man had ever desired her. Not Oliver. Not even Albert from Accounting, who'd asked her on a date a few months ago, then stood her up for some playoff game.

But there was heat in Stavros's gaze as he moved her in his arms.

"You don't love my cousin," he whispered, tightening his hold on her. "Admit it. He was just a dream you had to keep you warm at night."

Could it be true? How she wanted to be convinced! "How can you say that?"

His sensual lips curved. "Because as little as I know about love, it seems to involve really knowing someone, flaws and all. And you don't even know him."

She rolled her eyes. "I've worked for him for

three years. Of course I know Oliver. I know everything about him."

"Are you sure?" Stavros said, glancing at the dancing couple.

Following his gaze, Holly saw Oliver give a flirtatious smile to a pretty girl over his wife's shoulder. She saw Nicole notice, scowl, then deliberately step on her new husband's foot with her wicked stiletto heel.

"So he's a little flirty," she said. "It doesn't mean anything."

Now Stavros was the one to roll his eyes. "He sleeps with every woman he possibly can."

"He never tried to sleep with me," she protested.

"Because you're special."

Holly sucked in her breath. "I am?"

"Get that dying-cow look off your face," he said irritably. "Yes, special. His secretary before you filed a sexual harassment suit against him. I told Oliver if that ever happened again, I'd fire him, cousin or not. And he's a Minos man to the core. Like he said, selfish to the bone. Why would he want to risk losing an amazing secretary slaving away for him night and day, just for some cheap sex he can—and does—get everywhere else?"

"Cheap!" Holly had never even been naked with a man before. How dare Stavros imply she offered cheap sex to all comers? She glared at him. "What right do you have to criticize him? You're just as bad. You sleep with a new actress or model every week!"

Stavros's jaw tightened. "That's not true…" Then something made the anger drain out of his handsome face, replaced by stark, raw emotion. "But you're right. I have no right to criticize him. And I wouldn't, except he's trying to take your life. Don't let him do it," he said fiercely. He pulled her closer, looking down at her as they swayed to the slow music. "Oliver is using you. Look past your dream. See him for the man he really is."

Looking back at Oliver, now arguing with his new bride as they left the dance floor, Holly suddenly thought of all the times that he'd stopped her as she left the office on Friday nights, putting stacks of files into her arms. "You don't mind taking care of this over the weekend, do you, Holly?" he'd say, flashing her his most charming, boyish, slightly sheepish grin. "Thanks, you're the best!"

She thought of all the times he'd mysteriously disappear when an unpleasant conversation was required, leaving Holly to do his dirty work for him. And not just work like firing someone. Frequently she'd be left alone to sort out weeping, heartbroken women who appeared at the office, begging to see him, railing about broken promises.

At the time, Holly had convinced herself it was proof of his faith in her that he'd relied on her to handle such important matters.

But now...

She looked at Oliver and Nicole, who'd gone back to sit at the head table. There was still a smudge of white frosting on her sister's cheek. Earlier, when they'd cut the wedding cake, Nicole had delicately fed her new husband his slice, holding the pose beautifully for pictures. Immediately afterward, Oliver had smashed the piece into his bride's face to make the crowd laugh.

Now, sitting on the dais, they were arguing fiercely over champagne. She was trying to pull the bottle away from him. Yanking it back, Oliver tilted back his head and vengefully drank it straight from the bottle.

And this was supposed to be the happiest day of their lives.

Holly's body flashed hot, then cold, from her

scalp to her toes. With an intake of breath, she looked up at Stavros as they danced. "My sister—"

"She's made her bed. Now she'll have to lie in it." His hands tightened as he said, "But you don't have to."

Holly desperately tried to remember the feelings she'd once had for Oliver, all the lonely nights she'd spent in her tiny apartment, with only her romantic fantasies about her boss to keep her warm. But those memories had disappeared like mist against the cold reality of this wedding, and the hot feel of Stavros's hand over hers. The dream was gone.

"Why are you forcing me to see the truth?" she said helplessly. "Why do you care?"

Stavros abruptly stopped dancing. He looked down at her, his black eyes searing through her soul.

"Because I want you, Holly," he said huskily. "On my arm. In my bed." His hand trailed through her hair and down her back as he whispered, "I want you for my own."

He was going to hell for this.

Or at the very least, his conscience warned, he shouldn't hire her as his secretary. Because as hard as he'd tried to ignore her beauty—he *couldn't*.

Stavros looked down at her. Her emerald eyes widened. Her curly red hair looked like fire tumbling over her shoulders. Her petite body felt so soft and sensual in his arms.

But he wanted to keep her as his secretary. He wanted to keep her for everything. He wanted Holly more than he'd ever wanted anyone.

Why her? He didn't know. It couldn't just be her luscious beauty. He'd bedded beautiful women before.

Holly Marlowe was different. The supermodels and actresses seemed as glittery as tinsel, cold as snowflakes. Holly was real. She was warm and alive. Her heart shone from her beautiful green eyes. She didn't even try to guard her heart. He could read her feelings on her face.

And her body…

As they'd danced, he'd watched the tight red fabric slide against her ripe, curvaceous body, and his mouth had gone dry as he'd imagined feeling her naked skin against his own. With his hand against her lower back, he'd felt her hips move, felt the sway of her tiny waist. He'd watched her blush and shiver at his touch, and wondered how innocent she might be. Could she even be a virgin?

No. In this day and age? Surely not.

And yet he'd known then he had to make Holly his, if it was the last thing he did. Which it well could be.

His gaze fell to her pink lips, tracing down to her low-cut neckline, where with each sharp rise and fall of her breath he half expected the red fabric to tear, setting her deliciously full breasts free. He repeated huskily, "I want you."

Holly gave a sudden jagged intake of breath. "How can you be so cruel?"

Frowning, Stavros pulled back. "Cruel?"

"All right, so I'm just a secretary. I'm plain and boring and nothing special. That gives you no right to—no right to—"

"To what?" he said, mystified.

"Make fun of me!" Her voice ended with a sob, and she turned and fled, leaving him standing alone on the dance floor.

A low curse twisted his lips. Make fun of her? He'd never been more serious about anything in his life. Make fun of her? Was she insane?

Grimly, he turned through the crowd, trying to pursue her. But other people suddenly blocked his path on the dance floor, business acquaintances desperate to ingratiate themselves, women hoping for a shot at dancing in his arms.

He barely knew what he said to them as his eyes searched the crowds for Holly. His heart was racing and his body was in a cold sweat. Symptoms of his condition? His body shutting down?

All the things he'd never get the chance to do...

All the things he'd never thought of...

His eyes fell on Oliver, chatting with a trashy-looking girl by the open bar. As much as he despised his cousin's boorish behavior, Stavros realized in some ways he'd been just like him.

He'd never cheated or lied to a girlfriend, it was true. But that was hardly an amazing virtue when Stavros's relationships rarely lasted longer than a month. Whenever the pull of work became greater than the pull of lust, or if a mistress demanded any emotional involvement from him, Stavros would simply end the affair.

For nearly two decades, he'd worked eighteen hours a day, building his tech company. Unlike Oliver, he wasn't afraid of hard work. At first, he'd only wanted to succeed as a big middle finger to his estranged father, who'd cut off his mother without a penny and excluded Stavros from the Minos fortune. But by the time he was twenty, he'd learned the pleasures of work: the intensity, the focus, the thrill of victory. He'd become addicted to it.

But the truth was, he still wasn't so different from Oliver. Like his cousin, Stavros had spent all his adult life focusing on money and power and sleeping with beautiful women, while avoiding emotional entanglement. Stavros had just been better at it.

It was a blow for him to realize that Oliver, as weak and shallow as he was, had managed to do something he hadn't: he'd taken a wife.

Two years younger, and Oliver was already ahead. While Stavros had so little time left…

His eyes narrowed when he finally focused on Holly, speaking urgently with the bride on the other side of the ballroom. "Excuse me," he said shortly, and began pushing through the crowds, ignoring anyone who tried to talk to him.

He came up behind Holly just in time to hear the bride tell her angrily, "How dare you say such a thing!"

Holly flinched, but her voice was low as she pleaded, "I'm sorry, Nicole, I'm just scared for you…"

"I don't care what you imagine, or what Stavros Minos says. Oliver would never cheat. Not on me!" Nicole lifted her chin, her long white veil fluttering as her eyes flashed. "You don't deserve to be my maid of honor. I should have asked Yuna, not you! Better an old college roommate than a jealous old maid of a sister!"

"Nicole!"

"Forget it." Her sister's eyes sparkled as coldly as her tiara. "I want you out of here."

Holly took a deep breath. "Please. I wasn't trying to—"

"Get out!" Nicole shouted, loud enough to be heard over the orchestra, causing everyone nearby to turn and look.

Holly's shoulders flinched. She took a deep breath, then slowly turned away. Stavros had a brief glimpse of her stricken face before she walked through the silent, staring crowds.

He turned to Nicole.

"Your sister loves you," he said in a low voice. "She was trying to warn you."

"Warn me?" Nicole's perfect pink lip curled as she lifted her chin derisively. "Excuse me. I've never been so happy."

Stavros stared at her in disbelief.

"Good luck with that," he said, and went after Holly.

He found her shivering in front of the hotel, hopelessly trying to wave down a yellow taxi in the cold, snowy evening. As Christmas Eve deepened, the traffic on Central Park South had dissipated, leaving the city strangely quiet, tucked in to sleep beneath a blanket of snow, as the stars twinkled in the black sky.

When Holly saw him coming out of the hotel, her expression blanched. Turning, she stumbled away, across the empty street toward wintry, quiet Central Park. When he followed her, she shouted back desperately, "Leave me alone!"

"Holly, wait."

"No!"

Stavros caught up with her on the sidewalk near an empty horse carriage, festooned with holly and red bows, waiting patiently for customers. He grabbed her shoulder.

"Damn you…"

Then he saw her miserable face. Choking back his angry words, he pulled her into his arms. She cried against his chest, and he felt her shivering from grief and cold.

"I told her too late. I should have seen… I should have warned her long ago!"

"It's not your fault." Inwardly cursing both his

cousin and her sister, Stavros gently stroked her long red hair until the crying stopped.

She looked up at him, her lovely face desolate, tearstained with streaks of mascara as she wiped her eyes. "I'm not going back."

"Good."

She took a deep breath. "Nicole didn't send you after me?"

Stavros shook his head.

Her shoulders sagged for a moment, then she lifted her chin. "So what do you want?"

He came closer, looking down at her as scattered snowflakes whirled around them on the sidewalk in front of the dark, snowy park. "I told you."

Her eyes widened, and her lips parted. Then she turned her head sharply away. "Don't."

"Don't what?"

"Just don't." She swallowed hard, her green eyes glistening with tears as she looked at him beneath the moonlight. "All right, I was a fool over Oliver. I see now it was just a dream to stave off loneliness." Her voice broke. "But you don't have to be cruel to prove your point. I know I'm not your type, but I do still have feelings!"

"You think I'm toying with you?" Searching

her gaze, he said quietly, "I want you, Holly. As I've never wanted anyone."

Looking away, she mulishly shook her head.

As she shivered, he took off his sleek black tuxedo jacket and draped it gently over her shoulders. Reaching out, he cupped her cheek, running the tip of his thumb over her tender, trembling lower lip. "Holly, look at me."

Her eyes were huge in the moonlight as she flashed him a troubled glance. Behind her he could see the snowy park stretching out forever beneath the wintry, starlit night. She said haltingly, "You can't expect me to believe—"

"Believe this," he whispered. And, grabbing the lapels of the oversize tuxedo jacket around her, he pulled her hard against him, and swiftly lowered his mouth to hers.

CHAPTER THREE

EVEN IN HER wildest dreams, Holly had never imagined a kiss like this.

The few anemic kisses she'd had in her life, the forgettable ends of unsatisfying dates in high school and her one semester of college, had been nothing like this.

But then, she'd never been kissed by a man like Stavros.

His lips moved expertly as his tongue swept hers, taking command, taking possession. Held fast against his powerful, muscular body, she felt herself respond, felt her body rise.

Beneath his passionate, ruthless embrace, a spark of desire built inside her to a sudden white-hot flame.

She'd never felt like this before. The memory of her childish infatuation with Oliver melted away in a second beneath the intensity of this fire. A moment before, she'd been heartsick and despondent over her sister's harsh words. But now, she was lost in a sensual dream, her whole body tight with a sweet, savage yearning she never wanted to end.

When he finally pulled away, Holly looked up at him in shock. Behind him, the bright lights of Midtown skyscrapers illuminated his dark hair like a halo.

"Agape mou," he said hoarsely, stroking the edge of her cheekbone gently with his thumb. "You are everything I want in life. Everything."

Her throat went dry. Trying to smile, she said unevenly, "I bet you say that to all the girls."

"I've never said it to anyone." He looked toward the park's black lace of bare trees against the sweep of moonlit snow. "But life doesn't last forever. I can't waste a moment." He looked at her. "Will you?"

She bit her lip, feeling as if she was in a dream. "But you could have anyone you want. I'm so different…"

"Yes, different. I've watched you. You're warm and loving and kind. And so damned beautiful," he whispered, running a hand through her long red hair. His gaze dropped to her low-cut red dress. "And so sexy you'd make any man lose his mind."

Sexy? *Her?*

He cupped her cheek, kissing her forehead, her cheek, her lips, with butterfly kisses. Drawing back, he looked at her. "You're the only one I want."

Lowering his lips to hers, he kissed her again until she forgot all her insecurity and doubts, until she forgot her own name.

When he released her, she was still lost in the heat of his embrace. Lifting his phone to his ear, he said unsteadily, "Pick me up on Central Park South."

"You're leaving?" she whispered, oddly crestfallen.

"I'm taking you home."

"You don't need to take me home. I have my MetroCard. I can—"

"Not your home." His eyes burned through her. "To mine."

The thought of going home with him, of what that could mean, caused her to shiver as images of unimaginable delights filled her mind. Her breathing quickened. "Why?"

His sensual lips quirked at the edges. *"Why?"*

"I mean…do you need something typed, or…?"

"Is that all you think you are?"

She blushed beneath his gaze. She bit her lip,

then forced herself to respond. "You want to seduce me…?"

"How clearly must I say it?" he said huskily. He cupped her cheek, searching her gaze. "I want you, Holly. In my bed." He ran his hand through her hair as he whispered, "In my life."

And those three last words were the most shocking of all.

She stared at him. Once, she'd thought that working all hours and having a secret crush on her boss was the most she could expect out of life. Even earlier today, as she'd watched Oliver marry her little sister, Holly had been sure her future would be one of self-sacrifice, self-abnegation, caring for others, trying to ignore her own loneliness and misery.

Now, in Stavros's arms, wrapped in his tuxedo jacket, looking up at the handsome Greek billionaire's hungry black eyes, she felt like she'd suddenly traded a small black-and-white dream for a big Technicolor one.

His hand tightened on her shoulder. "Unless you still think you're in love with Oliver."

Holly took a deep breath, then slowly shook her head. In all her years working for Oliver, she'd seen only what she wanted to see: his boyish good looks, his cheerful, sly charm. She'd deliberately chosen to be blind to the rest: the laziness, the constant womanizing. "You were right," she said quietly. "It was just a ridiculous dream."

Stavros exhaled. "Then come home with me tonight."

"I can't…" Her heart was pounding. "I've never done anything like that."

"You've played by the rules for your whole life. So have I." His jaw tensed with an anger she didn't understand as he looked up toward the moon, icy and crystalline in the frozen black sky. "The tycoon's playbook. Dating models whose names I can barely remember now. Working twenty hours a day to build a fortune, and for what? To buy another Ferrari?" His lips twisted bitterly. "What has my life even been for?"

Holly stared at him, shocked that Stavros would allow himself to appear so vulnerable in front of anyone. It threw her into confusion. She'd thought of him as her all-knowing and powerful boss. But now, she realized, he was also just a man. With a beating heart, like hers.

"You're not giving yourself enough credit." Gently, she put her hand over his. "You've created jobs all over the world. You've built amazing tech that—"

"It doesn't matter. Not anymore."

"It matters a lot…"

"Not to me."

She took a deep breath. "Then what does?"

"This," he said simply, and lowered his lips to hers.

This time, his kiss was gentle and deep, wistful as a whisper. Could this really be happening? Was she dreaming? Or could she be totally drunk on half a glass of champagne?

Her heart filled with longing as his powerful body enveloped hers.

"Come home with me," he murmured against her lips.

She sucked in her breath, looking up at his handsome, shadowed face. "It's Christmas Eve…"

His dark gaze burned through her. "There's no one else I'd rather have in my arms when I wake on Christmas morning." His hand slowly traced down her cheek to the edge of her throat to her shoulder shivering beneath the oversize tuxedo jacket. "Unless you don't want me…"

Her—not want *him*? Just the ridiculousness of that suggestion made her gasp. "You can't think that…"

His shoulders relaxed, and his dark eyes met hers. "Then live like we're alive."

Live like we're alive. What a strange thing to say.

He was right, she'd followed the good-girl playbook her whole life, Holly thought suddenly. What had being sensible and safe and good ever done for her, except to leave her working overtime for free for a manipulative boss and sacrificing all her dreams to spoil her little sister—only to feel used and taken for granted by both?

"Say yes," Stavros urged huskily, stroking his hands slowly through her hair. "Come away with me. Be free."

A Rolls-Royce pulled up to the curb. She looked at him, her heart pounding.

"Yes," she breathed.

A trace of silvery moonlight caressed the edge of his sculpted, sensual lips as he drew back to make sure she meant it. "Yes?"

"Let's live like we're alive," she whispered.

Glancing back at the waiting car, he held out his hand. "Are you ready?"

Holly nodded, her heart pounding. But as she took his hand, she didn't feel ready. At all.

As she sat next to him in the back of the limo,

she barely noticed the driver in front. She didn't notice anything but Stavros beside her. The journey seemed like mere seconds before they pulled in front of a famous luxury hotel in Midtown.

"This is where you live?" Holly said, looking up at the skyscraper.

He smiled wryly. "You don't like it?"

"Of course I do, but…you live in a hotel?"

"It's convenient."

"Oh." Convenient? She supposed her shabby one-bedroom walk-up in Queens was convenient, too. She only had to change trains once to get to work. "But where is your home?"

He shrugged. "Everywhere. I travel a lot. I prefer not to keep permanent live-in staff."

"Right." She nodded sagely. "I prefer that, too."

His lips quirked, then he turned back toward the glamorous hotel, all decorated and sparkling with Christmas lights.

"Mr. Minos!" a uniformed doorman called desperately, rushing to hold open the door. "Thank you again. My wife hasn't stopped crying since she opened your Christmas card."

"It was nothing."

"Nothing!" The burly man swore under his breath. "Because of your Christmas gift, we can finally buy a house. Which means we can finally start trying to have a baby…" His voice choked off.

Stavros briefly put his hand on the burly man's shoulder. "Merry Christmas, Rob."

"Merry Christmas, Mr. Minos," he replied, unchecked tears streaming down his face.

Holding Holly's hand tightly, Stavros led her through the gilded door into the luxurious lobby, which had at its center an enormous gold Christmas tree decorated with red stars stretching two stories high. All around them, glamorous guests walked, some briskly and others strolling, many trailing assistants and bodyguards and holding little pampered dogs. But Holly only looked at the dark, powerful man beside her.

"That must have been some Christmas gift."

"It was just money," he said shortly, leading her through the lobby.

"The doorman—did he do a big favor for you or something?"

As he led her to the elevator, he gave an awkward shrug that made him look almost embarrassed. "Rob holds the door for me. Always smiles and says hello. Sometimes arranges for a car."

"And for that, you bought him and his wife a house?"

Pushing the elevator button, Stavros said again, "It was nothing. Really."

"Nothing to you," she said softly as the door slid open with a ding. "But everything to them."

Wordlessly, he walked into the elevator. She followed him.

"Why did you do it?"

"Because I could."

The same reason he offered me a job as his secretary, she thought. "Stavros," she said, "is it possible that, deep down, you're actually a good guy?"

She saw a flash of something bleak in his dark eyes, quickly veiled. He turned his face toward the sensor then pressed the button for the penthouse. "I'm a selfish bastard. Everyone knows that."

But there was something vulnerable in the tone of his voice. "I'm finding it hard to believe that. Unless there's something else," she said slowly. "Something you're not telling me. Is there—"

Her voice cut off as Stavros pressed her against the elevator wall, and hungrily lowered his mouth to hers.

He kissed her with such hot demand that the

questions starting to form in her mind disappeared as if they had never been. All that was left was heat. She felt molten with desire.

With a ding, the elevator door slid open.

Gripping her hand, he pulled her forward. Knees still weak, she followed, looking around her.

The enormous, starkly decorated penthouse was dark except for the white lights glittering from a ten-foot fresh-cut Christmas tree, which stood in front of the floor-to-ceiling windows overlooking the sparkling lights of the city below.

Still shivering from the intensity of his kiss, she looked at him. "Nice tree."

Stavros glanced at it as if he hadn't noticed it 'til now. "The hotel staff arranged that."

She looked around the apartment. There were no photographs on the walls. Nothing personal at all. The white-and-black decor looked like something out of a magazine, curated by a museum. "Did you just move in?"

"I bought this place five years ago."

She looked at him, startled. "Five *years*?"

"So?"

Holly thought of her own shabby walk-up apartment, filled with photos of family and friends, her comfortable, beat-up old furniture, her grandma's old quilt, the tangled-up yarn from her hopeless efforts to learn how to knit. "It seems unlived in."

"I hired the top designer in the city." He sounded a little disgruntled. "It's a look."

"Um." She bit her lip, then turned with a bright smile. "It's nice."

He pulled her into his arms. "You don't really think that."

"No." Butterflies flew through her belly as she stared at his beautiful mouth. Her gaze fell to his thick neck above his black tuxedo tie, to his broad shoulders in the white bespoke shirt, down all the way to the taut waistline of his black trousers to his powerful thighs. Butterflies? The crackle in her core felt more like the sizzle of lightning, burning through every nerve.

"Tell me the truth."

Biting her lip, she said, "I think your apartment is horrible."

"Better," he breathed, and he lowered his mouth to hers.

She tasted the sweetness of his mouth, and surrendered to the strength and power of his larger body wrapped around hers. Surrendered? She hungered for more.

Stavros kissed her for hours, or maybe just minutes, holding her body tightly against his as they stood in his shadowy, stark penthouse, beside the lights of the Christmas tree.

Heart pounding, dizzy from his passionate embrace, she pulled away with a shuddering breath. "This doesn't seem real."

"Lots of things don't feel real to me right now." Brushing tendrils of red hair away from her face, he said softly, "Except you."

As he pulled her tight against his body, his tuxedo jacket fell off her shoulders, dropping silently to the floor. His hands ran slowly through her hair and down her back, over her red dress.

Pulling away, her eyes fell to the floor as she warned him, "I don't have much experience."

"You're a virgin."

Her cheeks flamed. "How did you know?" she whispered. "Is it the way I kissed you?"

"Yes. And the way you shiver when I pull you into my arms. The first time I kissed you, I felt how new it was to you." He gently stroked her cheek, down the edge of her throat, to her breast. Her hard nipple ached even at that slight brush of contact. "That made it new to me, too."

Thinking of the gossip about his previous mistresses, all gorgeous sophisticated women no doubt with amazing, gymnastlike sexual skills, she suddenly couldn't meet his eyes. She bit her swollen lip. "What if I don't please you?"

With a low laugh, he gently lifted her chin as he countered, "What if I don't please you?"

"Are you crazy?" Her eyes went wide. "That's impossible!"

His lips twisted with an emotion she couldn't quite identify.

"That's how I feel about you, Holly," he said in a low voice. "You deserve better."

Stavros felt like *she* deserved better—better than the most famous Greek billionaire playboy in the world? But as she looked into his dark eyes, she saw he believed every word.

With a deep breath, she said quietly, "I can't work for you, Stavros. Not after this."

His expression fell. "You can't?"

Shaking her head, she gave him a crooked smile. "It's all right. Working for the VP of Operations won't be so bad."

His jaw tightened. "As you wish. You will, of course, still get your raise."

"I wouldn't feel comfortable—"

"Nonnegotiable." He cut her off. "You've more than earned it by being the company's hardest-working employee for years. In fact, you should be *demanding* a raise, not just accepting it. Damn it, Holly, you need to realize your value…"

Impulsively, she lifted up on her toes and kissed him. It was the briefest of kisses, feather-light, but it felt daring and terrifying to make the first move. As she started to draw back, he caught her, pulling her against him urgently. He kissed her hungry and hard, as if she was a life raft, and he was a drowning man.

Her body felt tight with need. Her breasts felt heavy, her nipples aching, sending electric sparks rushing through her every time they brushed against his hard chest. Tension coiled low and deep inside her, and she wanted him even closer. Reaching up, she pulled his head down harder to deepen the kiss.

With a growl, he lifted her up into his arms, and carried her down the hallway to an enormous bedroom.

The room was huge, but as sparsely decorated as the great room. Shadows filled the room, with a white gas fire shimmering like candlelight in the stark modern fireplace. Next to the windows, an artificial white tree gleamed with white lights.

Setting her down beside the bed, Stavros stroked her cheek. "You're so beautiful, Holly," he whispered. "I never imagined anyone could be so beautiful. Like an angel."

"I'm no angel."

He paused, looking at her in the winter moonlight flooding in through the window. "No." Reaching around her, he slowly unzipped her red maid-of-honor dress. "You're all woman."

Noiselessly, the dress dropped to the floor. Leaving her standing before him in only a bra, panties and high-heeled shoes.

She should have felt cold, standing nearly naked in front of him in the large bedroom. But beneath the heat of his gaze, she felt lit with an intoxicating fire as he slowly looked her over, from her full breasts plumped up by the white silk demi bra, past the softly curved plane of her belly, to her white silk panties, edged with lace. Taking her courage in her hands, she lifted her gaze.

Cupping her face in both hands, he lowered his head to hers and kissed her until the whole world swirled around her as she was lost in the sweet maelstrom of his embrace. His hands roamed feather-light over her body, stroking her breasts, her tiny waist, her big hips, the full curve of her backside. When his hands stroked over the silk bra, she held her breath until he reached around her to unhook the clasp, springing her free. With an intake of breath, he cupped her breasts, tweaking her taut nipples. She shuddered, vibrating with need.

Reaching down, he pulled off her high-heeled shoes, one by one, sending each skittering across the black floor. Pushing her back against the white comforter of the king-size bed, he undid the cuff links of his shirt.

Never taking his eyes off her, he loosened the buttons, and she had her first flash of his hard chest. He dropped the shirt to the floor, and she got her full view of it, in all its tanned, muscular glory. A trail of dark hair led to his flat, taut belly.

He unzipped his dark trousers, and slowly pulled them down his thighs, along with his underwear, revealing his muscular, powerful legs laced with more dark hair. She sucked in her breath as he straightened, and she saw how big he was, and how hard for her.

She wasn't a total innocent. She'd seen pictures of the male form. There had been that sex education course in high school, gag gifts in shops, and working in an office, she'd once stumbled over a coworker watching porn on his computer. She wasn't totally naive.

But in this moment, seeing him naked in all his physical power and brute force, she felt nervous. Swallowing, she pulled the white comforter up to her chin, squeezing her eyes shut, suddenly shaking.

She felt the mattress move beneath her.

"Holly." His voice was low. His hand, warm and gentle, was on her shoulder. "Look at me."

Biting her lip, she looked up at him, wondering what she should do, what she should say. Stavros's darkly handsome face was intense, lost in desire.

"Are you afraid?" he asked in a low voice.

Biting her lip, she looked away. "I don't want to displease you. I—I don't know what to do."

"Holly," he repeated huskily. Slowly, he ran a fingertip down her bare shoulder above the comforter. Just that simple touch caused a sizzle of electricity to go through her. "Look at me. All of me. And see if you please me."

She looked down as he'd commanded, and saw how large he was, how hard and thick and smooth. He wanted her. There could be no doubt of that.

Trembling, she lifted her mouth toward his. Holding her tenderly, he kissed her.

With his lips on hers, all rational thought disappeared again in molten heat, in the rising need that made her forget everything else. She was dimly aware of the comforter disappearing. As his naked body covered hers, as she felt his weight and strength on her, she sighed with pleasure and a sense of rightness—of being part of something, half of a whole. Entwining her tongue with his own, he teased her, toyed with her, made her gasp. The kiss was so perfect, so deep, when he pulled away she was left with a sense of loss and longing.

He nibbled her chin, then slowly worked his way down her naked body with hot kisses, as his hands caressed her bare skin. He licked her neck, her collarbone. He cupped her full, bare breasts and lowered his mouth slowly to the valley between them, making her grip the white cotton sheet beneath her as she felt his hot breath against her skin.

He wrapped his lips around her taut, aching nipple. His mouth was wet and hot as he suckled her, pulling her deep into his mouth, swirling her with his tongue. She gasped with pleasure, closing her eyes.

He moved to the other breast, suckling that nipple in turn, as his hands stroked slowly down her body, caressing her belly, her hips, her thighs. He lowered his head, kissing where his hands had just caressed her, seducing her with feather-light touches that made her skin burn. She felt his fingertips lift the edge of her panties from her hips.

"Do you want me?" he whispered, his voice so low it made her tremble.

"Yes," she breathed.

"Louder."

"Yes!" she cried, her cheeks burning.

Then Stavros suddenly pulled away, looking down at her. And he spoke words she'd never expected. Words that nearly made her heart stop.

"Marry me, Holly." Stavros cupped her cheek, his dark eyes burning in the Christmas-Eve night. "Have a child with me."

Her eyes widened with shock. "Are you serious?"

"I've never been more serious."

Holly couldn't believe it. Even a one-night stand with a man like Stavros seemed like a dream. But he wanted to marry her? Have a baby with her?

Tears came to her eyes.

"I've shocked you," he said grimly.

"No...yes." Lifting her chin, she whispered,

"It's like all my most impossible dreams are suddenly coming true."

Exhaling, he ran his thumb lightly along her cheekbone, brushing a tear away. "Is that a yes?"

"Yes," she breathed.

He smiled, and it was brighter than the sun, even as she saw a suspicious sheen in his black eyes. "You'll never regret it. I swear it on my life."

"I'll do my best to make you happy…"

"You already have." Lowering his head, he kissed her. "I want you, *agape mou*," he groaned against her lips. "I'll want you until the day I die."

She held her breath as he kissed down her throat, to her breasts, then her belly. She shivered, lost in a sensual dream. He wanted to marry her. He wanted to fill her with his child…

He slowly pulled her white silk panties down her legs, and tossed them away. Kneeling between her legs on the bed, he pushed her thighs apart. She felt the warmth of his breath against the most sensitive part of her body, a place no man had ever touched.

Lowering his head, he spread her wide with his hands. For a moment, she couldn't breathe, as he teased her with the warmth of his breath.

Then he tasted her, delicately with the tip of

his tongue, swirling against the core of her pleasure. Even as she gasped in shock at the intensity of the sensation, he moved, deepening his possession, reaching around her to hold her tight, as he lapped her with the full width of his tongue.

She cried out, grasping the bed beneath her as electricity whipped through her, causing her back to arch, lifting off the mattress.

He moaned, his hands tightening on her thighs, holding her down as her whole body strained to fly. Her breasts felt tight, her whole body aching with need. Then he pushed a single thick fingertip inside her, stretching her.

Pleasure built inside her, whirling her in every direction, pleasure she'd never imagined. She held her breath, closing her eyes as her head tilted back. Her body arched off the bed as he worked her with his tongue—then, just as she tightened with pleasure almost too great to bear, he pushed a second fingertip inside her. And she exploded into a thousand chiming diamonds, in a million colors, soaring through the sky.

She was only dimly aware as he reached for a condom from a nearby nightstand. But as he started to tear it open, she covered it with her hand.

"No," she panted, still dizzy beneath waves of pleasure.

"No?" He looked stunned.

"You don't need that." She smiled. "Live like you're alive."

Savage joy lit up his dark eyes as he threw the condom to the floor. "This is my first time without one," he whispered, lowering his head to kiss her. "My first time ever."

"For both of us," she breathed, closing her eyes with a delicious shiver as he gently bit the corner of her neck. Prickles of desire raced through her body.

"I'll end the pain as quickly as I can," he said huskily.

Pain? What pain? All she felt was bliss—

Gripping her hips, he positioned himself between her legs. In a swift, deliberate movement, he sheathed himself deeply inside her.

She gasped as he broke the barrier inside her. But he held himself utterly still, holding her as the sudden pang of pain lessened, then disappeared. His weight was heavy on hers, his hard-muscled chest sliding sensually over her breasts as he lowered his head to kiss her, gently at first, then with rising passion as she started to return his embrace.

Only then did he slowly begin to move inside her, thrusting deeper, inch by inch. And to her shock, a delicious new tension began to coil, low and deep inside her belly.

Reaching up to his shoulders, Holly pulled him down tighter against her, wanting him deeper, wanting more. Wanting everything.

CHAPTER FOUR

HE WAS ALREADY deep inside her, so deliciously deep. Stavros fought to keep control as she gripped his shoulders, pulling his naked body down against her. He felt her move beneath him, tightening with new desire.

"Yes," she'd whispered. He shuddered at the memory.

When Holly had told him she'd marry him and have his child, that single word had nearly unmanned him. And now it was almost impossible to hold himself back, when just the feel of her and the sight of her were enough to make him explode. Especially when he was bare inside her, a pleasure he'd never experienced before. He was a breath from losing control.

But he couldn't. Not yet. He set his jaw, desperately trying to keep hold of the reins in a ruthless grip.

Stavros felt like a virgin himself.

He'd spoken the forbidden words that seared

his heart, words he'd never said to any woman. Outlandish words, asking her to marry him and have his baby. It was his one last chance to leave something of himself behind. An adoring wife, and a son or daughter to carry on his name.

She should have refused him, laughed in his face. After all, they were barely more than strangers to each other.

Instead, she'd accepted him, as if she'd dreamed her whole life of marrying Stavros and having his child.

All he'd wanted to do was possess her, to thrust inside her, hard and fast. But he'd known the first time would be painful for her. So he'd forced himself to go slow, to take his time, to seduce her. To make it good for her.

When he'd first pushed himself inside her, he'd hated to see sudden pain wipe out the joy in her beautiful face. So he'd held her, until her pain passed, though it was total agony to hold himself still, so hard with need, so deep inside her. But he managed it—for her. He'd kissed her sweaty forehead, her soft cheek, and held her close until he felt her shoulders relax, and a sigh came from her lips.

Now, the raw intensity of his desire for her was almost too much to bear. As he felt her move beneath him, her every gasp of pleasure was pure torture.

She was soft, so soft. And so sensual. He was on a razor's edge of control.

Holly Marlowe was a sensual goddess. He wondered how he hadn't recognized her beauty and sensuality from the moment he'd first seen her, three years before. He should have seen past the mousy bun and baggy, unflattering clothes. He should have known what they really were—a disguise.

She was his now, and she would be his for as long as he lived. She would be his wife. He would fill her with his child—

With a shudder of need, he kissed her lips, tenderly at first, then with building passion. As her hands gripped his shoulders, pushing him tighter against her, he panted with need, beads of sweat rising on his forehead as he continued to thrust slowly, gently, letting her feel every inch of him moving inside her.

The pleasure was incredible. Some of his control began to slip. But he wasn't ready for it to end, not yet. He wanted to make it amazing for her.

He looked down. Holly's face was sweetly lifted, her eyes closed with ecstasy. He almost exploded right then. With a shudder, he gripped her hips and slowly began to increase his pace. Her lips parted as she sucked in her breath, her fingernails raking slowly down his naked back.

When he finally felt her tighten around him as her gasp of pleasure turned into a scream, he could hold himself back no longer. He plunged deep into her, and his own hoarse shout melded with hers, echoing against the windows overlooking the sparkling lights of the city. The white tree twinkled amid the dark shadows of the bedroom, as the clock struck midnight on Christmas Eve.

When Stavros woke, the soft light of dawn was coming through his bedroom's floor-to-ceiling windows. Outside, the wintry city looked gray on Christmas morning.

He'd been lost in the best dream he'd ever had. Holly had been kissing him, and she'd been heavily pregnant. Emotion shone from her vulnerable eyes as she'd told him she loved him—

Now, he looked at the soft, warm woman in his arms. Both of them were still naked beneath the white comforter. He realized he'd slept all night, holding her in his arms. They were still facing each other, their foreheads almost touching on the pillow, her curly red hair stretched out behind her. Even in sleep, his arms had been wrapped protectively around her.

I love you, Stavros, she'd whispered in the dream, her heart and soul in her eyes.

It was just a dream, he reminded himself harshly. Totally meaningless. But in the cold light of reality, he felt her imagined words like an ice pick through his soul. *I love you.*

When he'd imagined leaving her behind after his death, he'd pictured a pregnant wife dressed in black, standing stoically beside his grave.

He hadn't thought of how it might feel to be the widow left behind. How Holly's warm, generous, loving heart might react to all that grief. It could destroy her.

Could? It *would*.

His conscience, buried and repressed for so long, suddenly came out in full force. Could he really be so selfish? Was he a Minos man through and through after all?

I'll leave her all my fortune, he argued with himself.

But Holly wouldn't care about that, not really. After all, she'd spent three years working for Oliver without asking for the raise and promotion she deserved. When she'd walked into his twenty-million-dollar penthouse, with its elegant decor created at great expense by Manhattan's foremost interior designer, she'd been left utterly unmoved.

Holly, alone of all women on earth, didn't seem to give a damn about money.

So his billions would bring her little pleasure. Far from it. With her kind, sympathetic heart, his widow's fortune would make her an easy target for unscrupulous fortune hunters. First and foremost: his greedy cousin and her spoiled sister.

Stavros looked back at Holly, sleeping so sweetly and trustingly in his arms.

I'll leave her with a child, he tried to tell himself. That, at least, was something he knew she wanted.

But a child she would raise alone?

He felt sick. He'd seduced Holly under false pretenses. His dream had only shown the stark truth: he'd soon make her love him. He'd already started to make her care. Her heart was innocent; she had no defense against love, not like Stavros. Only he knew what love really meant: surrender or possession. Being the helpless conquered or tyrannical conqueror. No one came out of it unscathed.

Just the fact that she'd convinced herself, even for a moment, that she could love a man as unworthy of it as Oliver only proved how open her heart was. She was not guarded. She had no walls.

So when Stavros died, which he would before next Christmas, he would not leave behind him a dignified wife in a black veil and chic black mourning suit standing stoically beside his grave, as he'd imagined.

Instead, he'd leave a broken woman, bewildered and lost, perhaps with a child to raise on her own. For all he knew, she might already be pregnant. Stavros would soon be dead and buried, forgotten. But Holly would remain, a widow with a broken heart, bitterly cursing him as the liar who'd seduced her with false promises of forever and changed her life in ways she'd never imagined.

A razor blade lifted to his throat as he looked at her, still sleeping trustingly in his arms. He had no choice. He had to tell her the truth. Explain about his fatal brain tumor before it was too late for her to change her mind about marrying him.

If it wasn't already too late.

"You're awake." Holly's voice was soft and

warm as she drowsily opened her eyes, smiling up at him with love shining from her face. "Merry Christmas."

Stavros looked down at her. His lips parted to choke out the truth. Then he stopped.

He suddenly realized with horrifying clarity that even if he told her about his illness *she would marry him, anyway.*

As that sister of hers had said, taking care of other people was what Holly did best. She gave and gave and gave, leaving nothing for herself. From the time her parents had died, she'd put her little sister first. From the moment she'd started working at Minos International, she'd put Oliver first. She sacrificed herself for others, even if they didn't deserve it.

And if Stavros told her he was dying she would do the same for him. She'd take care of him. She'd hold his hand through chemotherapy appointments. She'd love him. She'd never leave him.

Even if it destroyed her.

"Holly," he said hoarsely, struggling to know what to do, "there's something you need to…"

He felt a sharp pain behind his right eye, so sudden and savage he jerked back from her. The bed seemed like it was swaying beneath him.

Holding the comforter over her chest, Holly sat up with a frown. "Stavros?"

The pain was nearly blinding, spreading through his head, causing a rough throbbing in his skull. He put a trembling hand against his forehead. How long did he have? Even his doctor had hedged his bets when he'd given him the news two days before.

"No one can say for sure how long you'll live, Mr. Minos," Dr. Ramirez had said gravely. But when Stavros had pressed him, he'd admitted six to nine months might be typical for a patient at his advanced stage.

But Stavros wasn't a typical man. He'd always prided himself on it. He'd always beaten others, proving himself stronger and smarter and faster. His tumor was part of him. All his worst sins bottled up into one fleshy mass rapidly spreading through his brain.

"What is it?" Holly cried. "What's wrong?"

Slowly getting out of bed, he stood still, blinking until the blurriness passed and he could see again in the dim early light of his penthouse's master bedroom. Wearily, he stumbled across the room, opened a drawer and pulled on some loosely slung knit pants. He felt as if he was a million years old.

Going to the wall of windows, he stared out at the cold gray city beneath him. So very cold. So very gray.

All these years he'd hated his father as heartless and cruel. All these years he'd despised his cousin as a selfish bastard.

What Stavros had just done proved him to be the worst of them all.

He was dying, so in a pathetic attempt to make his life matter, to be important to someone other than his shareholders, he'd proposed marriage to this trusting girl. He'd taken her virginity. That was bad enough.

But he'd wanted to do so much more.

He'd wanted to crush her heart and spirit and make her suffer with him as he declined, and failed, and died. Clinging to her like a drowning man, like a filthy coward, he'd wanted to drag her down with him.

Most women he knew might have been happy to exchange six months of holding his hand and watching him die for a vast pot of gold at the end. Those women guarded their souls—if they even *had* souls.

But not Holly. He'd seen it in her warm, trusting face. From the first moment he'd taken her arm at her sister's wedding, when they'd danced at the reception, when he'd first kissed her in the snowy darkness of Central Park, he'd seen how quickly her opinion of him had changed, from resentment, to curiosity, to bewildered desire. And finally, when she'd opened her eyes just now in the gray light of Christmas morning in his bed, he'd seen the way her soft emerald eyes glowed. And he'd known.

He could break her.

"Stavros, you're scaring me." From behind him on the bed, the tone of her voice suddenly changed, becoming artificially bright. "You've changed your mind about marrying me, haven't you? You're scared to tell me. But don't be. I wouldn't blame you if—"

"Yes." His voice was harsh as he turned to face her. "I've changed my mind."

"You have?"

Her lovely face went pale, but she spoke the words as if this was exactly what she'd expected all along. As if she'd known her joy and ecstasy could only be a brief fantasy.

Setting his shoulders, forcing himself not to feel, he said shortly, "Last night was a mistake."

Holly's shoulders sagged, and she looked away, toward the twinkling white tree. Holding the comforter over her naked breasts, she whispered, "Was it something I did, or…?"

"I was drunk last night," he lied harshly, knowing the fastest way through this was to hit her at her most vulnerable point, so she wouldn't fight it. One hard painful wrench, and it would all be over. "I mean—" he shrugged, the stereotype of a casually cruel playboy "—let's face it. Like you said, you aren't my usual type."

The blow hit her squarely. The last color drained from her cheeks, leaving her pale as a ghost beneath her fiery hair. She swallowed, tried to speak, failed. She was lost in pain and insecurity and couldn't see past it. Wordlessly, she looked down at her hands, clasped together tightly over the comforter. "I…"

"You should go," he said coldly.

Not meeting his eyes, Holly slowly got out of bed. Picking up her bra and panties, and her crumpled red gown from the floor, she covered her amazing body. Her face held the pure, unmitigated heartbreak of youth, and he hated himself at that moment more than he'd ever hated anyone. Which was saying something.

"My driver will take you home. He could stop at the drugstore, if you like."

"What for?"

"Emergency contraception," he said coldly.

"That's not necessary."

"It's not?"

Stepping into her high-heeled shoes, she lifted her chin. With a deep breath, she looked back at him. "I told you. I can take the subway."

His stomach churned at the bleakness in her eyes. "Holly—"

She cut him off with a harsh gesture. Then she gave a forced smile. "It's my fault. I knew all along you couldn't possibly— I never should have come here."

Holly was apologizing...to him. It took all of Stavros's willpower not to reach for her, pull her into his arms, tell her how he was to blame for everything. But the habits of a lifetime held him in good stead. His hands tightened into fists at his sides. "I'll make sure you still get the promotion and raise you deserve," was all he said. "But it's better we don't work together in the future."

"Yes." Looking back at him, her eyes suddenly glittered with a strange ferocity he'd never seen before. "You're right. Goodbye." She turned away.

But he couldn't let her go, not like this. Not when he suddenly wondered if he'd ever see her again.

Stavros grabbed her arm. "Wait."

"What else is there to say?" she asked, her voice catching.

His fingers tightened over her wrist. Last night had been the most incredible sexual experience of his life—and more than sexual. Their eyes locked, and all Stavros wanted to do was pull her back into his arms. Into his bed. Into his life.

But not at the cost of hers.

He dropped her wrist.

"It's unlikely you're pregnant after just one night. But if anything happens," he drawled, "you'll let my lawyers know, won't you?"

Her lips parted in confusion. "Your lawyers?"

"Yes. If you're pregnant, they'll take care of it."

Her face went white, then red. Then her green eyes narrowed with cold fury. "You're too kind."

Stavros had played the part of a coldhearted, womanizing louse to perfection, insinuating that he would have his lawyers pay her off if there was a child. Insinuating he was too busy and important to even be bothered with such a minor detail.

No wonder she was now looking at him as if he was the most despicable human being on earth.

"That's all." He tilted his head, making his eyes as frozen and gray as the world outside. "Now get out."

With an intake of breath, Holly said in a trembling voice, "I wish I'd never met you."

And turning on her heel, she left his penthouse, taking all the warmth and light with her, leaving Stavros alone in the coldest Christmas he'd ever known.

CHAPTER FIVE

Eleven months later

HOLLY PAUSED IN shoveling snow, taking a deep breath that turned to smoke in the chill air. All around her, sunshine illuminated the snow, making the white blanket sparkle like diamonds.

It was the day after Thanksgiving, and for the first time in her life, she was spending it alone—and in Switzerland, of all places. Farther from home than she could ever have imagined last Christmas, when her heart had been so savagely broken.

She leaned against the shovel. A soft smile lifted to her face as she looked toward the porch. But she wasn't alone, not truly. She'd never be alone again.

Late November snow was nearly four feet deep around the winding path that led from her tiny chalet, just a rustic cabin really, to the sliver of main road. The nearest village was a mile away, tucked in a remote valley of the Swiss Alps, and even that was nearly deserted in winter. The nearest real market town was Zedermatt, where the festive outdoor Christmas market would open today. A friend had begged her to accompany him there this afternoon. Somewhat hesitantly, she'd agreed. Why not enjoy the season?

Holly's days of working long hours in an office, always filled with stress and urgency, now seemed like a strange dream from long ago. Here, there was only tranquility and peace, and of course, snow, but she'd gotten used to that, shoveling the path to her door every day, and listening to the quiet sound of snowflakes each night against the slanted roof.

In the last year, everything had changed. Her old life in New York, the person she'd once been, were all gone. So much lost. But even more gained.

A baby's gurgle came from the small porch of her chalet, and Holly looked up tenderly, with a familiar joy in her heart.

"Are you hungry, sweet boy?" Shoveling the last few scoops of wet snow from the path to the road, she carried the shovel back toward the chalet. She tromped her winter boots heavily to knock off the snow, then climbed the steps to the porch and smiled down at her sweet two-month-old baby, Freddie, named after her own beloved father.

The baby gurgled and waved his arms happily, at least as much as he could do, bundled up as he was in a one-piece winter fleece that covered him from mittens to hood, tucked snugly into the baby seat with a blanket over the top.

"We'll get you fed," Holly promised, smiling. Setting down the shovel nearby, she lifted the baby seat's handle and carried him inside.

Inside the rustic cabin, a fire blazed in the old stone fireplace. This chalet was two hundred years old, with low ceilings braced with hand-hewn wooden beams. The furniture wasn't quite as old, but close. And the place was tiny: there was only one bedroom. But every day since she'd arrived here, pregnant and heartbroken, last February, she'd blessed her former employer, who'd offered her free lodging in exchange for keeping an eye on the place.

Coming inside, Holly set down the baby carrier then pushed the door closed behind her to keep out the frozen air. She yanked off her heavy winter coat and colorful hand-knitted hat, hanging them on the coat rack while she shook errant snowflakes out of her long red braid. Pulling off her boots, she left them on towels placed just inside the door and stepped nimbly into the room, wearing a loose green sweater and snug black leggings ending in thick warm socks.

Unbuckling Freddie out of the carrier, she changed his diaper then wrapped him snugly in a soft baby blanket. Cradling him in her arms, she carried him to the worn sofa near the fire. As she fed the baby, he looked up at her with big wondering eyes, nestling his tiny hand between her breasts.

Holly had arrived here in a panic in February, wondering how she'd ever cope with raising a child on her own. Then she'd remembered: she already had. She'd raised her baby sister when Holly was barely more than a child herself.

After Stavros had coldly thrown her out of his bed last Christmas morning, she'd never gone back to her job at Minos International. She hadn't even gone back to collect her carefully tended plant or framed photos of her sister. A friend had collected them for her, along with her last check.

Holly had had money in her savings account. She'd learned to be careful with money the hard way, at eighteen, when she'd found herself with a little sister to raise and very little money from her parents' life insurance to support them. Ever since, she'd always been careful.

That saved her when, in mid-January as she'd started her job search, she'd discovered the real source of the stomach flu she hadn't been able to shake: she was pregnant.

And the memory of Stavros's words in bed on Christmas morning chilled her. *If you're pregnant, let my lawyers know...they'll take care of it.*

That, more than anything, had destroyed any lingering illusions she'd had about Stavros Minos being a decent human being.

She'd, of course, heard stories about men lying to get a woman into bed. But she'd never imagined it would happen to her. When he'd desired her, Stavros had been romantic beyond belief, seducing her with sweet words, passionate kisses and, most astonishing of all, proposing marriage and having a child together.

But from the moment he'd gotten what he wanted, he'd expected her to disappear.

Holly had known she wouldn't let him make the baby disappear, too. She couldn't take the risk of seeing Stavros Minos again, even accidentally, or letting him know she was pregnant.

So she'd left New York.

She'd been happy in Switzerland. She was lucky. All right, so Thanksgiving, the traditional American kickoff to the Christmas season, had felt a little quiet yesterday, since the holiday wasn't celebrated in Switzerland. Growing up, Holly's mother had always spent the whole day cooking turkey and baking pies that smelled heavenly, while the two girls stretched out in the morning on the carpet of the family room, watching the Thanksgiving Day parade on TV. In the afternoon, during commercials of his football game, their father inevitably wandered into the kitchen, hoping to sneak a taste of mashed potatoes and cranberry sauce, before their mother shooed him away with a playful smack of a Santa-decorated towel.

Christmas had always been Holly's favorite time of year. At least until last year. Now, with her heartbreaking memories of Stavros last Christmas Day, she was almost afraid to face the holidays this year.

Holly steadied herself. She had so much to be thankful for now. This warm, cozy chalet, her baby, her health. And after nearly a year of estrangement, when she'd phoned her sister to wish her happy Thanksgiving yesterday, for the first time her sister had actually answered the phone.

All right, so Nicole had mostly just yelled at her during the ten-minute call. Apparently Oliver had been fired from three different jobs over the past year, causing the newlyweds to move from Hong Kong to Los Angeles, then back to New York, where he was now unemployed. Her sister blamed Holly.

"It's your fault," Nicole had shouted. "His bosses expect too much. You should be here taking care of things for him. And for me!"

Feeling guilty, Holly tried to change the subject. "I've been busy this year, too…" And she'd finally told her sister the happy news about the baby.

But if she'd hoped it would make Nicole forgive her, or have any joy at the news of a baby nephew, Holly was soon disappointed.

Her sister had been shocked, then furious, then demanded to know the identity of the father. Swearing her to secrecy, Holly had shivered as she'd whispered Stavros's name into the phone. It had been the first time she'd spoken his name aloud in almost a year.

But knowing that secret only seemed to enrage Nicole more.

"So now you're a baby mama for a billionaire?" she'd cried. "You selfish cow—you never have to worry about anything, do you?"

And her sister had slammed down the phone.

At least they were talking again, Holly told herself now, trying to remain cheerful. It was a start. And who knew what the future could hold? After all, they were coming into the season of miracles.

Her baby was the biggest miracle of all. She could never be sad about anything for long, not when she had him. She smiled down at Freddie, who was all bright eyes and plump cheeks. And if, with his dark eyes and black hair, her baby strongly resembled a man she didn't want to remember, she blocked it from her mind with harsh determination.

Freddie was hers. He had no father. Holly would be the only parent he'd ever need.

The baby, born a week late in a Zurich hospital, had been over four kilos—nine pounds, two ounces—and continued to gain weight at a healthy clip. As Holly looked down at her precious child, her heart twisted with love such as she'd never known.

And Stavros would never even know he existed.

Holly looked into the fire. She'd had no choice,

she reminded herself fiercely, as she'd done many times over the past year. Stavros had made his feelings clear. The morning after he'd seduced her with promises and lies, she'd woken up on the happiest Christmas morning she'd ever known, only to be tossed out with the trash.

After she'd found out she was pregnant, she'd fled New York in fear that his lawyers might try to force her to end the pregnancy. She'd gone to London, where her former employer had made it clear she had a standing job offer. He'd been bewildered when, instead of accepting a high-paying office job, she'd asked about being a caretaker to his family's old chalet in Switzerland.

"It's not St. Moritz, you know," he'd replied doubtfully, stroking his white beard. "The village is deserted in winter. It was my great-grandfather's cabin. It's a bit of a wreck. Are you sure?"

Holly had been sure. And she'd never regretted her choice. She'd made friends with her elderly neighbors down the road, kind people who'd delighted in showering lonely, pregnant Holly with advice and *Älplermagronen*, and since her baby's birth, with babysitting offers and cake. Holly's high-school German was rapidly improving.

As far as she was concerned, she'd be happy to live here forever. Happy enough.

How could she ever admit she felt lonely sometimes, or that she didn't think her heart would ever completely heal from her brief affair with Stavros? It would be the height of ingratitude to ever feel sad, when she had so much: home, friends and Freddie.

It was enough. It had to be enough.

She looked down at the sleeping baby in her arms. Stroking his rosy cheek, her heart full of love, she whispered, "I'm going to make your first Christmas perfect, Freddie. See if I don't."

The baby yawned in reply, drowsy and sleepy with a full belly and a warm fire. Carefully, Holly rose to her feet and settled the baby into a small bassinet in the cabin's bedroom. Leaving him in the darkened room to nap, she softly closed the door behind her.

Back in the main room, the fire crackled. Untying her braid to shake her hair free, she went to the closet and dug to the back, where she found a large box.

It was time to reclaim Christmas.

Reaching into her family's old box of treasures, Holly pulled out her grandmother's old quilt, the chipped ceramic Santa cookie jar, a garland of colorful felt stars and the Christmas recipe book with her mother's faded handwriting. Vintage ornaments from her childhood. She touched the hand-knitted stockings, and her heart lifted to her throat.

She decorated the small main room, putting the ornaments on the wooden mantel above the fire, and then stepped back to look. That would have to do, at least until she got a tree at the Christmas market. A lump rose in her throat. She'd make sure Freddie had a wonderful Christmas—

There was a hard knock at the door, making her jump. Then she shook her head, smiling. Who was it? Elke with freshly baked gingerbread? Horst, offering to shovel snow? Brushing off some errant Christmas glitter from her black leggings, Holly opened the door.

And her smile dropped.

"Holly." Stavros's coldly handsome face glowered down at her. His voice was low, barely more than a growl.

Her lips parted in a silent gasp.

"Is it true?" he demanded. Moving closer, he narrowed his eyes, black as night. His jawline was dark with five-o'clock shadow, and his powerful form filled the door, all broad shoulders and muscle. Behind him, parked on the edge of the snowy road, she saw his driver waiting inside a black luxury SUV that looked totally out of place in this rural Swiss valley.

Terror went through her. Her baby. He'd come for her baby! Instinctively she started to close the door in his face. "I don't want to see you—"

"Too bad." Reaching out a powerful arm, he blocked the door, and pushed his way inside.

Shivering with sickening fear, she stepped back as he closed the door behind him. He calmly shook the snowflakes from his Italian cashmere coat.

He was even more handsome than she remembered. Even more dangerous.

"I heard a rumor." Stavros looked slowly around the cabin, with its roaring fireplace and homemade Christmas decorations. Pulling off his black leather gloves, he tucked them into his pockets and turned to her with narrowed eyes. His voice was colder than the frigid winter air outside. "Is it true?"

"Is what true?" she whispered, with a sinking heart.

Stavros's jaw was tight as he looked right through her. "Did you have my baby, Holly?"

Her blood went cold. Teeth chattering, she

stared at him. The man who'd once seduced her, who'd wooed her with words and languorous kisses, was now looking at her with hatred in his eyes.

She tried to laugh. "Where did you hear that?"

"You're a terrible liar," he said softly. "Is it possible you've lied to me for nearly a year?"

Her heart lifted to her throat. It was all she could do not to turn and rush into the bedroom, to grab their sleeping baby and try to run before it was too late.

But it was already too late. She'd never outrun Stavros. Especially with his driver outside. There was no escape.

Her mouth went dry as she tried to think of a lie he might believe. Something, anything. She could say Freddie was another man's son. Stavros knew she'd been a virgin in his bed, but maybe she'd slept with someone else right afterward. A hookup after Christmas! A drunken one-night stand on New Year's Eve! Anything!

But as her eyes met Stavros's, she couldn't force any lie from her trembling lips.

"Who told you?" she whispered, her voice barely audible.

Stavros staggered back, his dark eyes wide. For a split second, he did not move.

Then he took a deep breath. Reaching out, he cupped her cheek. She felt the rough warmth of his palm against her skin. His touch was tender, but his expression was cruel.

"Who told me? Oliver. Who heard it from your sister." He said softly, "He enjoyed telling me. He's never been able to make me feel like a fool before." Blinding sunlight from the window, amplified by the snow, suddenly bathed the hard edges of his cheekbones and jawline in golden light. "But he's not to blame. You are."

Shivering, she licked her lips. "I…"

"You promised to tell me if there was a pregnancy." His dark eyes were aflame with cold fury. "You're a liar, Holly. A filthy, despicable liar."

But at that, sudden rage filled her, chasing away the shadows of fear.

"*I'm* a liar?" she said incredulously.

His lip curled scornfully. "You hid your pregnancy and ran away like a thief—"

Holly was past listening as nearly a year of grief and rage exploded from her heart.

"*You're* the liar, Stavros. When you wanted me in your bed, you promised the sun and the moon! You asked me to marry you!" Her body shook with pain and anger. "But as soon as you were done, you couldn't throw me away fast enough on Christmas morning!"

He started to speak, then abruptly cut himself off. He looked away, his jaw clenching. He said in a low voice, "I had a good reason."

"Yeah, right!" Holly, who'd never lost her temper in her life, truly lost it now. "You'd had your fun and you were done. You didn't care what it did to me. You're selfish to the bone. Why would I ever let a man like you near my son?"

"Son?" He slowly turned to her. Then his eyes narrowed. "I want to meet him."

"No."

"I'm his father."

"Father?" She lifted her chin incredulously. "You're a sperm donor, nothing more. I don't want anything to do with you. We're better off without you." She jabbed her finger toward the door. "Now get out!"

Stavros clawed his hands through his dark, tousled hair. His black eyes looked weary, almost bleak. "You don't understand. I wasn't myself last year—"

"You were exactly yourself," she interrupted coldly. "The lying, coldhearted bastard everyone else claimed you were." Holly was surprised he'd even bother trying to make excuses.

It didn't seem like his style. But it didn't matter. She wouldn't let herself get suckered into caring about him ever again. She shook her head. "You're selfish and cruel. Just like Oliver said— Minos men only care about themselves!"

Abruptly, Stavros turned to face her.

"I was dying, Holly," he said flatly. "That's why I sent you away on Christmas morning. I thought I was dying." He narrowed his eyes. "And now I want to see my son."

Stavros wasn't prepared for the shock he'd felt, seeing her in the doorway of the Alpine chalet.

He was even less prepared for the shock of learning that the rumor was true, and he was a father.

A father. And the baby had to be around two months old. All those months of the pregnancy, and he hadn't known. He felt dizzy with the revelation.

Dizzy, and angry. But not just at Holly.

So much had happened over the last year. He'd been unusually emotional last Christmas, convinced he'd been about to die. That must have been why he'd acted so foolishly, seducing her with such wild longing, proposing marriage, even begging her to have his child.

It embarrassed him now to remember it. All that rank sentimentality, the desperation he'd felt for love and family and home.

Thank God, he'd recovered from that, along with the cancer. Holly Marlowe was nothing to him now.

Or so he'd thought. But now they had a child together. That meant they'd be linked forever, even after death.

And looking at Holly now, Stavros felt the same punch in the gut that he remembered from last Christmas. If anything, she looked more beautiful, more impossibly desirable.

Her curly red hair tumbled over her shoulders of her soft green tunic, and the angry pant of her breath showed off breasts grown fuller and even more womanly than he remembered. Tight leggings revealed the delicious shape of her hips and backside. Her emerald eyes sparkled with fury as they narrowed in disbelief.

"Dying?" she said incredulously.

"It's true. Last Christmas I thought I only had months to live."

He waited for her to react, but her face was stony.

"Didn't you hear me?" he demanded. She shrugged.

"I'm waiting for the punch line," she said coldly.

"Damn you. I'm trying to tell you something I haven't shared with anyone."

"Lucky me."

Turning away, Stavros paced, staring briefly at the crackling fire in the fireplace, then out of the frosted window toward the sun sparkling on the snow. He took a deep breath. "I had a brain tumor. I was told I was dying."

"And that inspired you to seduce me and lie to me?"

"Dying inspired me to want more," he said softly. "To make one last attempt to leave something behind. A wife. A child." He turned back to her. "That's why I slept with you, Holly. That's why I said I wanted to marry you and have a child with you. I wasn't lying. I did want it."

She clenched her hands, glaring at him. "So what happened?"

"I couldn't go through with it. I couldn't be that selfish. I knew you would fall in love with me. You were so…innocent. So trusting. I didn't want to break your heart and make you collapse with grief after I died."

She pulled back, looking strangely outraged. He'd forgotten that about her, how she wore her emotions so visibly on her face. Most people he knew hid their emotions behind iron walls. Including and especially himself, notwithstanding Christmas Eve last year, which he still tried not to think about.

"So you said those horrible things," Holly said, "and sent me away for my sake. You're such a good guy."

Her tone was acid. Staring at her in shock, Stavros realized he'd taken her innocence in more ways than one.

He'd kept the secret of his illness entirely to himself for a year. Even when his hair had fallen out, he'd shaved his head and pretended it was a fashion choice. When his skin had turned ashy and he lost weight, he'd blamed it on the stress of mergers and acquisitions.

Until this moment, only his doctors had known the truth. Literally no one else. Stavros had thought, if he ever opened up to Holly about that night, he would be instantly forgiven. Because, damn it, he'd been *dying*.

He'd obviously thought wrong.

"Why didn't you die, then?" Holly said scornfully. She tilted her head in mild curiosity, as if asking why he'd missed breakfast. "Why didn't your tumor kill you?"

Stavros thought of the months of painful treatment, getting radiation and chemotherapy. After he'd abandoned his dream of leaving behind a wife and child, he'd decided to give up his dying body to an experimental new therapy. He'd thought he might at least benefit science by his death.

Instead, in August, he'd been informed by shocked doctors that the inoperable tumor had started to shrink.

Now, Stavros shrugged, as if it didn't matter. "It was a miracle."

Holly snorted. "Of course it was." She rolled her eyes. "Men like you always have miracles, don't they?"

"Men like me?"

"Selfish and richer than the earth."

The scorn in her voice set his teeth on edge. "Look, I'm getting a little tired of you calling me selfish—"

"The truth hurts, does it?"

"Stop trying to put all the blame on me," he growled. "You're the one who has kept my son from me. I told you to contact my lawyers if you were pregnant!"

"I wasn't going to let you force me into having an abortion!"

Shocked, Stavros stared at her, his forehead furrowed. "What?"

"Christmas morning, you told me you'd changed your mind. You didn't want a child. You said if I was pregnant, I should contact your lawyers and they'd *take care of it*!" An angry sob choked her voice. "Did you think I didn't know what you meant?"

Furious, he grabbed her shoulders. "I *meant* I'd provide for my child with a great deal of *money*," he growled. "Damn you!"

As Holly stared at him, Stavros abruptly dropped his hands, exhaling.

Finally, he understood. Since Oliver had phoned him yesterday, he'd wondered how it could be true. Why would Holly not tell him about a pregnancy? Was it some kind of nefarious attempt at revenge for his seduction and subsequent rejection? Holly had apparently kept the news from her sister as well. She'd only told her yesterday, obviously knowing Nicole would tell Oliver and he'd tell Stavros. But why?

Now it was clear. Holly had been afraid. He gritted his teeth at that insult. But now, with her baby safely born, she was ready to claim the fortune that was due her.

Stavros looked around the ramshackle old

cabin, saw the cracks between the logs where the cold wind blew. Holly was no gold digger, but any mother would want the best for her child. She was ready for them to live in greater comfort, and who could blame her?

Now that he understood her motivation, Stavros relaxed.

"You have nothing to worry about," he proclaimed. "I will provide for the baby, if he's mine."

"If?" she repeated in fury.

"I want to meet him."

Holly glared at him. "No."

Stavros blinked. "What?"

"You came here to find out if I'd had your baby. Fine. Now you know. Your lawyers probably gave you papers for me to sign. Some kind of settlement to make sure neither I nor my baby would ever make a claim on your full fortune."

"How did you know—" He cut himself off too late. She gave him a cold smile.

"I was a secretary for many years to powerful men. I know how you all think. You're no different from the rest." She came closer, her eyes glowing intently. "I don't want your money. I'll take nothing from you. And nothing is what you'll get in return. Freddie is mine. You will relinquish all parental rights."

"Relinquish?" he breathed in shock. All his earlier smug confidence had disappeared. Surely Holly couldn't hate him so much, when all he'd been trying to do last Christmas was protect her from her own weakness? There was no reason for her to toss him out like this, without even letting him see the baby. Unless—

A thought hit him like hard kick in the gut from a steel-toed boot.

"Is there another man?" he said slowly.

An odd smile lifted the corner of her lovely lips. "What difference would it make to you?"

"None," he lied coldly.

But against his will, he was enraged at the thought.

He'd spent the year as celibate as monk, exhausted after too many hours at the hospital alone, getting medical treatment that sucked away his life and energy. Why had he imagined, just because he'd taken her virginity, that a beautiful young woman like Holly would have spent the last year celibate as well?

For the last year, he'd tried not to think about her, or how out of control she'd made him feel last year. He'd told himself that he'd done the noble thing, the hard thing, setting her free. Since he'd gone into complete remission last month, he'd tried to forget that their night together had been the single greatest sensual experience of his life.

Because Holly made him lose control. She made him weak. He'd couldn't risk seeing her again.

Until he'd gotten the call from Oliver yesterday. Then he'd had no choice.

Because whatever Holly might think of him, Stavros would never abandon his child. Even if he wasn't sure he was ready to be a father, he would provide for him.

His lawyers had warned him if the baby rumor was true, he should immediately ask for a paternity test, and insist that Holly sign papers to recuse herself and her child from any other claim on his billions before he paid her a dime.

His lawyers had never told Stavros what to do if Holly scorned him, his money, and the horse he rode in on.

"You…don't even want my son to know me?" he asked.

She gave a single short shake of her head.

"So why tell me about the baby at all?" he said harshly. "Just to punish me?"

"I never intended for you to know. I swore my sister to secrecy."

Holly hadn't intended for him to know about his son? Ever? Shock left him scrambling. "But my son needs a father!"

She lifted her chin. "Better no father at all than someone who will let him down, and teach him all the wrong lessons about how to be a man. How to lie. How to make meaningless promises. How to be ruthless and selfish and care only about himself!"

Stavros hadn't thought he had much of a heart left, but her words stabbed him deep. He thought of his own childhood, growing up without a father. Having to figure out for himself how to be a man.

Hardly aware of what he was saying, he insisted, "But what if I want to be in his life? What if I want to help raise him?"

Holly's eyes widened.

Then her lips twisted scornfully. "I've heard that lie before."

"This is different…"

"You might have lured me once into some romantic fantasy. Never again." Crossing the cabin, she wrenched open the door. A blast of cold air flew inside, whipping the fire with its icy fingers. "Please go. Don't come back. Have your lawyers send me the papers." She looked at him coldly. "There's no reason for us to ever meet again."

"Holly, you're not being fair—"

It was the wrong word to use.

"Fair?" Turning, she called out to the driver parked in front of the cabin. "Your boss is ready to leave."

Stavros's head was spinning. He needed time. He hadn't even seen his baby, or held him in his arms. He wasn't sure what he wanted anymore. But Holly was already making the decision for both of them.

She didn't want any part of him. Not as a husband. Not as a father. Even his money wasn't good enough.

Fine, he told himself coldly. He'd keep his money. He didn't need her. Or their baby.

"Fine. You'll have the papers by the end of the day," he told her grimly.

"Good," she said in the same tone.

Stavros set his jaw, glaring at her. Then he stalked out of the cabin without a word, his long dark coat flying behind him as he breathed a Greek curse that left a whisper of white smoke in the icy air. The frozen snow crackled beneath his Italian leather shoes as he passed his waiting driver and got into the back seat of the Rolls-Royce Cullinan.

"Let's go," he growled to his driver.

"Where to, Mr. Minos?"

"Back to the airport," Stavros barked. He'd tried to take responsibility, but she didn't want him in their baby's life. Fine. He'd give her exactly what she wanted. He'd call his lawyers and have them draw up the new papers, severing his parental rights, and giving Holly absolutely nothing.

All my most impossible dreams are suddenly coming true.

The memory of her trembling voice came back to him, whispered into the silent, sweet night last Christmas Eve. Leaning his head back against the leather seat, Stavros closed his eyes, pushing away the memory. Along with how it had felt to have her body against his that sacred, holy night.

But as the Rolls-Royce wound its way back through the Swiss valley, his shoulders only grew more tense. He stared out at the picturesque valley, blanketed by white snow sparkling beneath the sun.

For the past year, he'd hidden his illness from everyone, driving himself harder at work, so no one would know his secret. When he'd gotten the shocking news that he was going to live, he'd been alone in the medical clinic, with no one to share the miracle except for doctors eagerly planning to document the case to medical journals and astonish their colleagues.

Was this how he would spend that miracle? Abandoning the woman he'd seduced last Christmas…and the child they'd conceived together? Leaving a son to grow up without a father, and would despise Stavros as a heartless stranger?

If he did, he truly was a Minos to the core.

His eyes flew open.

"Stop," he said hoarsely.

CHAPTER SIX

HOLLY PUSHED HER stroller through the festive Christmas market in Zedermatt's tiny town square.

Sparkling lights were festooned over outdoor walkways filled with locals and tourists bundled up against the cold, browsing dozens of decorated outdoor stalls, filled with charming homemade items, centered around an enormous Christmas tree in the square. Sausages of every kind, *bockwurst* and *knockwurst* and every other kind of *wurst*, sizzled on outdoor grills, adding the delicious salty smell to scents of pine, fresh mountain air and hot spiced wine called *glühwein*. Smiles were everywhere on rosy cheeks.

Past the eighteenth-century buildings around the square, including a town hall with an elaborate cuckoo clock that rang the time, craggy, snow-covered Alps rose above the tiny valley.

As she pushed her baby's stroller through the crowds, everyone was welcoming. Gertrud and

Karin, elderly sisters who ran a bakery in town, made a point of cooing over the baby. Gunther and Elfriede, selling scented homemade candles from their pine-decorated stall, generously praised Holly's improving language skills.

Holly was surrounded by friends. She'd made a home.

So why did she feel so miserable?

Stavros, she thought. Just his name caused her heart to twist. Seeing him had been more painful than she'd ever imagined. And more terrifying. Asking him to give up his parental rights to Freddie, she'd been shaking inside.

Why had she been so afraid? Even if he'd never actually meant to threaten her into terminating her pregnancy as she'd once feared, he'd still made his total lack of interest in fatherhood clear.

So if he'd seemed hurt by her words, it must have only been his pride, injured at being told he wasn't wanted. Obviously. What else could it be?

Dying inspired me to want more. To make one last attempt to leave something behind. A wife. A child. That's why I slept with you, Holly. That's why I said I wanted to marry you and have a child. I wasn't lying. I did want it.

Was it true? Had he really been dying?

She hadn't believed him at first. But a proud man like Stavros Minos wouldn't lie. Not about something like that, something that exposed weakness.

Holly's hands tightened on the stroller handle. It didn't matter. She wasn't going to let herself feel anything for him, ever again. Even if he'd thought he was dying, it was no excuse for how he'd treated her—seducing her, abandoning her!

But if he'd really thought he had only months to live…

Her heart twisted. What must that have been like for an arrogant tycoon to be helpless, facing death? What was it like for a powerful man to feel so powerless?

He'd kept his illness secret. She was the first person he'd told. He'd obviously thought it would make her forgive him.

But even if her traitorous heart might be tempted to feel some sympathy, how could she?

Because in spite of Stavros acting all shocked and upset that she'd never told him she was pregnant, he obviously didn't want to be a father. If he'd really wanted to be part of their son's life, he never would have let himself be scared off so easily today. He would have insisted on sticking around, whatever she said. But he hadn't.

As soon as she'd given him an escape route, and told him they wouldn't try to claim any part of his fortune, he'd been off like a shot.

She and Freddie were better off without him. They *were*. Stavros was selfish and coldhearted. She'd never give him the chance to hurt their son like he'd hurt her. She'd done the right thing, sending Stavros away. She should be relieved, knowing he'd never bother her or the baby again.

So why, when Freddie suddenly whimpered in his stroller, did Holly feel like doing the same?

"Here's your hot chocolate." Coming toward her with an eager smile, Hans Müller handed her a steaming paper cup. The young Swiss man was sandy-haired and solidly built, with pale blue eyes.

"Thank you," she said, turning to him with a smile. "You're too kind."

"I would do anything for you, Holly." He looked at her. "You know that."

Sipping her cocoa, she shifted uneasily. She'd met Hans six months before, in a local café. He'd wanted to improve his English skills, and she her German. Back then, she'd been heavily pregnant, and their friendship had been easy. But something had changed lately. She feared he wanted more from her than she could give. It made her feel guilty. It wasn't Hans's fault Stavros had crushed all her romantic illusions forever.

"Hans," she said awkwardly, lifting the pacifier from Freddie's blanket to put it back in the fussing baby's mouth. "You know you're very dear to me..."

"And you're dear to me. So is Freddie." He looked at the baby, now sucking contentedly in the stroller. He paused. "He needs a father." He looked at her. "You need a husband."

"I—I..." She took a deep breath. The last thing she wanted to do was hurt Hans, who'd been nothing but kind to her. *I don't think of you that way*, she prepared to say.

Then she stopped.

The only men she'd ever imagined as romantic partners had both been disasters—the three-year time-waster of imagining herself in love with Oliver, followed by the massive, life-changing fiasco last Christmas Eve with Stavros.

Maybe she should give Hans a chance. Maybe the fact that she was totally unattracted to him was actually a sign in his favor.

Because the only man who'd ever truly made her experience desire, who'd awakened her body and made her soul sing, had been a handsome, black-hearted liar who'd betrayed her before the sun rose on Christmas morning.

But as she looked at Hans's shining face, she knew she couldn't be that cruel. She couldn't destroy his illusions and ruin his life by letting him love her. Not when she knew she'd never love him—or any man—ever again.

Holly took a deep breath. It was hard, because she feared she'd lose his friendship. "I'm sorry, but you have to know—"

"Holly." The voice behind her was low and sensual. "Won't you introduce me to your friend?"

She turned with an intake of breath.

Stavros stood in the middle of the Christmas market, taller than anyone in the crowd, darkly handsome and powerful in his well-cut suit and cashmere coat. Her mouth went dry.

"What are you doing here?" she choked out. "I thought you were on your way back to New York—"

"Why would I leave?" Stavros's gaze fell longingly to the baby in the stroller. "When my son is here?"

"Freddie is your son?" Hans stammered.

He turned with a sharp-toothed smile. "Freddie?" He lifted a sardonic eyebrow. "Yes. I'm his father." He extended his black-gloved hand. "You are?"

"Hans… Hans Müller." Shaking Stavros's hand, he nervously glanced at Holly. "I didn't know Freddie had a father. No, of course, I know everyone has a father. That is to say…"

He looked around helplessly.

"Indeed," Stavros said, his expression amused. Then he looked at Holly. "We need to talk."

"I have nothing else to say to you," she said stonily. "I'm here with Hans. I'm not going to be rude and—"

But the young man was already backing away from the powerful, broad-shouldered tycoon. "It's all right—you both have things to talk about. He's your baby's father." He looked at Holly reproachfully beneath his warm hat. "You should have told me."

"I'm sorry…" Her mouth went dry. "I never meant to…"

Hans lightly touched the top of the baby's dark head, then said softly, *"Auf wiedersehen."*

And sadly, Hans disappeared into the crowd.

Stavros said behind her, "That's the man you replaced me with?"

Holly whirled on him. "He's a friend! Nothing more!"

"He wanted more." Stavros looked down at the baby bundled up in a blanket, sucking drowsily on his pacifier. Kneeling beside the stroller, he tenderly stroked the baby's plump cheek. "My son," he whispered. "I am here. I'm your father, Freddie."

Against her will, she felt a violent twist in her heart. She took a deep breath. "Why did you come back? I told you! We don't want you here!"

Rising to his feet, Stavros glanced to the right and left. From the sweet-smelling bakery stall next door, Holly saw Gertrud watching them with a frown.

Taking her arm with one hand and the stroller handle with the other, Stavros escorted her to a quiet spot on the other side of the massive, brightly decorated Christmas tree. His black eyes were cold. "Fine. You hate me. You don't care that I was dying. You don't want my money or anything to do with me."

"Exactly," she replied, pushing aside her feelings at the thought of him dying.

"Hating me doesn't give you the right to keep my son from me." Stavros looked down at the bundled-up baby, drowsing in the stroller as he sucked on his pacifier. "And whatever you say, I won't abandon him."

A chill went through her. "It's not your choice."

He smiled. "Ah, but it is," he said softly. "I'm his father. That means I have the right to be in his life. And I'm going to be. From now on."

She had no idea why he was pretending to care about Freddie. Out of a misguided sense of pride? Or just to hurt her?

But either way, he was correct. He did have rights, if he chose to fight for them. Fear gripped her heart as she faced him. "What do you intend to do?"

Stavros's expression was like ice. "I'm going to marry you, Holly."

Stavros hadn't intended to propose marriage like this. But it was logical. It was the best way to secure his son, and give the baby the future he deserved—with two parents in the same home.

When he'd returned to Holly's cabin an hour before, he'd intended to calmly insist on his parental rights, or perhaps threaten to sue for partial custody.

He'd arrived just in time to see Holly and the baby—dark-haired, tiny—climb into another man's car. And all his calm plans had gone up in smoke. He'd grimly had his driver follow them at a distance.

Meeting Hans in person at the Christmas market, Stavros was reassured that the man was no threat. Holly herself made that clear. There was no way the two of them had even kissed, for all the man's obvious interest in her.

But Holly was too bright, too beautiful, to be alone for long. As Stavros had watched her push the stroller through the Christmas market, her fiery red hair flying behind her, she'd looked effortlessly pretty in her black leggings and black puffy jacket. She smiled at everyone. And everyone smiled at her. She shone brighter than the star at the top of the Christmas tree.

He'd been mesmerized.

But he couldn't let her know that. He couldn't reveal his weakness. The one time he'd been weak enough to give in to foolish longings last Christmas, it had changed not just his life, but hers—permanent changes from a momentary whim.

He had a son. From the moment he'd seen his tiny, innocent baby, he'd known he would die to protect him. Just touching his cheek had made Stavros's heart expand in a way it never had before. He looked again at the sweetly drowsy baby in the stroller. He ached to take his son in his arms, but he'd never even held a baby before.

He didn't know how. But there was one thing he could do: give Freddie the home he deserved, by marrying his mother.

Stavros tightened his hands at his sides.

"Well?" he said to Holly coldly. "What is your answer?"

He waited, wondering what her reply would be. Any other woman would have immediately said yes, but then, Holly wasn't like any other woman. She clearly despised him and didn't want him in her life. On the other hand, she'd agreed to marry him last Christmas. There was an even better reason for her to agree to it now. They had a child.

She stared at him, her emerald eyes wide. Then she did the one thing he'd never expected.

She burst into laughter.

"What's so funny?" he said grumpily.

"You." She wiped a tear from the corner of her eye. "Thank you for that."

"It's not a joke."

"You're wrong." She shook her head. "Do you really think I'd agree to marry a man I don't trust?"

Stavros ground his teeth. He'd been reasonable. He'd explained about his illness. He'd told her he wanted to take responsibility. He'd even asked her to marry him. What more could he do to convince her? He said shortly, "I have never lied to you."

"You lied about your illness last year."

"Damn it, Holly, what should I have done? Let you wreck your life holding my hand, watching me die?"

Her jaw tightened. "You should have given me the choice."

"Like you're giving me now, trying to cut me out of Freddie's life? I'm his father!" He narrowed his eyes. "I want to give him a name."

"He has one. Frederick Marlowe."

"No."

"It's a good name. My father's name!"

"His last name will be Minos."

"Why are you pretending to care?"

"I'm not pretending." Coming closer, he tried not to notice how her eyes sparkled beneath the Christmas lights in the festive outdoor market in the town square, with the snowy Alps soaring above. "I'm going to give my son the life he deserves. Marry me, or face the consequences."

"Is that a threat?"

"I will be part of my son's life, one way or another."

Glaring at him, she lifted her chin. "I won't be

bullied into marriage. I don't care how rich or powerful you are. Family is what matters. Not money."

And as Stavros looked down at her in the cold mountain air, everything became crystal clear.

He had little experience managing tricky relationships. In the past, if a mistress ever got too demanding, he'd simply ended the relationship.

So think of it as a business deal. He coolly reassessed the situation. *A hostile takeover.* He looked down at the tiny dark-haired baby. He wanted to be a steady, permanent part of his child's life. Clearly, the best way to do that was to marry Holly. But she didn't want to marry him. She didn't want his money. She didn't want his name.

So how best to negotiate? How to win?

He could brutally fight her for custody. With his deep pockets, his lawyers would crush her. But inexperienced as Stavros was with long-term relationships, he didn't think this would ultimately lead to a happy home for their child.

How else could he get leverage?

Then he realized. She'd just revealed her weakness. *Family is what matters*, she'd said. And she'd shown that belief in every aspect of her life. She'd given up college and her own dreams, given up years of her life for that worthless sister of hers. She'd quit her job and fled to Europe when she'd thought she needed to protect her baby.

How could he use her own heart against her?

A sudden idea occurred to him. It made him feel sick inside. He tried to think of something else.

But Holly already looked as if she were ready to turn on her heel and stalk away, taking their child with her. He needed some way to spend time with her. To make her calm down and see reason. And he could think of only one way.

Since she was none too pleased with her sister at that moment, dragging her to New York wasn't an option.

But Freddie had a grandfather.

If Stavros tried to convince Holly that Aristides Minos deserved to meet the baby, he doubted her tender heart would resist. At least until she met the loathsome man. There was a reason Stavros despised his father to the core.

But a trip to Greece would give Stavros the time he needed to convince Holly to marry him. With any luck, he argued with himself, the old man wouldn't even be home.

Deliberately relaxing his shoulders, Stavros

gave Holly his most charming smile. "I don't want to fight with you."

"Fine." Suspicion creased her forehead. "But I still won't marry you."

"Of course you won't," he said easily, still smiling. "You don't trust me. Because I treated you so badly."

Her lips parted. Then she narrowed her eyes. "Whatever you're doing, it's not going to work. My answer's still no."

She was too intuitive by half. "All right. So let's talk about Freddie. And what's best for him."

Holly snorted. "A father, you're going to say. But he doesn't need a father like you, who's selfish and—"

"My own father is honest to a fault," he interrupted. "Doesn't he have the right to meet his grandson?"

That stopped her angry words. She closed her mouth, then said uncertainly, "You have a father?"

Stavros gave her a crooked smile. "As your friend Hans said, everyone has a father."

"But you've never mentioned him. I assumed he was dead."

"You assumed wrong." Stavros had just *wished*

his father was dead. Many, many times, after he'd divorced his mother and cut them off without a penny. After he'd ignored all of Stavros's frantic pleas for help when he was seventeen, and she'd gotten that fatal diagnosis. Pushing the awful memories away, Stavros said blandly, "I'm his only son." It was a guess. For all he knew, the man had ten other children he was ignoring or neglecting around the world. "Would you keep him from his only grandchild?"

Emotions crossed Holly's face. It was almost too easy to read her. First, she wanted to angrily refuse. Then he saw sympathy, and regret.

"Is he like you?" she said finally. "Your father?"

"He's nothing like me."

"No?"

"Like I said. He's honest to a fault." Aristides definitely was authentic, that was true. He never tried to be anything but who he was. Social niceties like courtesy and kindness were utterly unknown to him.

"Really?" Holly said doubtfully, looking at him.

Stavros gave a humorless smile. "Really."

He tilted his head, waiting for her answer. On the other side of the towering Christmas tree, he could hear jaunty, festive music played by a brass band. How strange it would feel to see his father after all these years.

If he did, he would feel nothing. It had all happened so long ago. Stavros was no longer the boy who'd desperately craved a father's love, and been ruthlessly rejected. He was strong now, untouchable, with a heart of stone.

Taking a deep breath, he exhaled a cloud of smoke in the cold air. The tension eased in his shoulders. Feeling nothing was what Stavros did best.

Holly glared at him, gritting her teeth. "Fine," she sighed. "He can meet the baby." She paused. "Where? When?"

"He lives in Greece, I'm afraid."

"Greece!"

He gave her a smile he didn't feel. "The Minos villa on Minos Island."

"You grew up on your own island?"

"Until I was eight." Pulling his phone from his pocket, he dialed his pilot's number before she could change her mind. "We'll leave at once. My jet is waiting."

"I can't just leave," she protested weakly. "I'm the caretaker of my old boss's chalet."

Covering the phone's mouthpiece as the pilot

answered the other end of the line, Stavros told her, "I'll handle it."

And he did. When she said their baby couldn't travel in the Rolls-Royce SUV without a baby seat, one miraculously materialized five minutes later. Before they'd returned to the chalet, where she packed an overnight bag for herself and the baby, Stavros had personally contacted the chalet's owner in London. The man sounded frankly astonished to get a direct call from the famous tech billionaire. "No one needs to stay there, really," he told Stavros. "It was empty for a year." And just like that, it was done.

"Does *everyone* do what you say?" Holly said resentfully as the SUV drove back over the winding road toward the private airport in St. Moritz. He lifted an eyebrow.

"Everyone but you."

"Everyone including me," she said softly, staring out her window at the snowy Alpine valley, with its picturesque, colorful chalets beneath sharp, brooding mountains. He watched her silently, hoping it was true.

She believed that they were heading to Greece for one night, which they were. What she didn't know was that, after their brief visit to his father's villa, Stavros intended to take both her and the baby back to live in New York.

He'd make her his wife. By any means necessary.

When they arrived at the tiny airport, his driver opened the SUV's door, then took their bags and folding stroller from the trunk. Holly carried the baby across the tarmac and up the air stairs to his new Gulfstream G650ER. As Stavros followed her, his gaze fell on the sweet curve of her backside in the snug black leggings, and he felt a flash of heat.

Eleven months. That was how long he'd been without a woman.

His night with Holly had been the most incredible sexual experience of his life.

She'd ruined him for all other women.

It was strange. He'd never thought of it in those terms. He'd assumed his lack of desire had been caused by radiation and chemotherapy treatments, while keeping up his workaholic schedule so no one would guess at his illness. Sex had been the last thing on his agenda.

But from the moment Holly had answered the door of that snowy chalet, her cheeks rosy and her sweater and leggings showing off her perfect hourglass shape, the whole past year of pent-up desire had exploded inside him with a vengeance.

Great, he thought resentfully. *Now* his libido chose to come alive? With the one woman on earth who seemed immune to him?

Or was she?

He looked at Holly, now sitting in an opposite chair inside the jet, as far away from him as possible, holding their baby in her lap.

The flight attendant appeared. "Would you like a drink, Mr. Minos? Your usual Scotch?"

Stavros's gaze remained on Holly, tracing the curve of her neck, her red hair curling down her shoulders, the fullness of her breasts beneath her loose sweater. Was she nursing, or had her breasts always been that big?

Holly looked up. "I'd like some sparkling water, please."

"Of course, madam. Sir?"

As Stavros looked at Holly, their eyes locked. The air between them sizzled. Images went through him of last Christmas, when she'd been naked in his bed. The heat of her body sliding against his own, her soft cry joining his hoarse shout as their mutual desire exploded. He was hard as a rock.

"Champagne," he said. "It's a celebration. A new start for us both."

Holly's eyes widened, her cheeks turning pink. Quickly, she turned her head away.

But it was too late. Because now he knew. In spite of her anger, in spite of her hatred, she was as sexually aware of him as he was of her.

And he suddenly realized there were additional benefits to taking her as his wife. Reasons that had nothing to do with taking care of their child.

He'd seduced her before. He would seduce her again. And this time, it would be forever.

CHAPTER SEVEN

SITTING IN A red convertible, as Stavros drove it down the coastal road clinging to the edge of the Aegean Sea, Holly looked out at the bright turquoise water. She felt the warm wind on her face. Felt Stavros's every move beside her. It was like torture. Holly's heart lifted to her throat.

Why had she ever agreed to this?

Guilt, she thought. Back in Switzerland, she'd convinced herself that however Stavros had betrayed her with his playboy ways and lying lips, her baby's grandfather was blameless. Now, she cursed the good intentions that had led her to come to this small Greek island.

Yes, she wanted Freddie to have a grandfather. Of course she did. She felt bad for the elderly man, who sounded like an honest, decent sort of person, to be stuck with such an obviously neglectful son as Stavros. He deserved to know he had a grandson.

Her motives hadn't been purely noble, it was

true. Some part of her had hoped desperately, after Stavros spent a little time with their baby, he'd grow bored with the care of parenting a child, and decide to give up custody, and leave them alone.

But being this close to Stavros was difficult. Holly threw him a troubled glance. Every time he'd tried to speak with her on the trip from Switzerland, she'd coldly cut him off. But her own feelings frightened her. The truth was, part of her still desired him. Part of her, a very foolish part, still held on to the dream of being a family.

She'd never be that stupid again, she told herself fiercely. And they'd only be on this Greek island a single night before she returned to Switzerland. What damage could a single night do?

Hearing her baby chortling happily in the convertible's back seat, she looked back and shivered. One night could change everything.

"Almost there," Stavros murmured beside her, glancing at her sideways. She felt a flash of heat.

"Is Greece always this warm in November?" she said in a strangled voice.

"It is warmer than usual." His sensual lips curved up on the edges, as if he knew exactly how his nearness was affecting her. He lazily turned the wheel with one hand, driving the luxury convertible down the twisting road with no effort at all. Her gaze lingered on his powerful forearms, laced with dark hair below his rolled-up sleeves.

It was just the sun making her hot, she told herself. As it lowered toward the western horizon, she felt too warm in the sweater and leggings she'd worn from Switzerland. Her feet were roasting in their leather boots. "I didn't pack any summer clothes."

"Don't worry." Stavros glanced at her, his eyes traveling over her. "It's been arranged."

"You always arrange everything," she sighed.

"My assistant contacted my father's housekeeper and let her know we were on the way. She will provide anything you or Freddie might need."

Her cheeks flamed. "Uh… Thanks. I guess." She tried to smile. "What did your father say when he heard about the baby?"

He shrugged. "I didn't tell him."

"What?"

"I haven't spoken to my father for twenty years."

"Twenty—" Her jaw dropped. "Did you even tell him we were coming to visit?"

Stavros's hand tightened on the steering wheel as he drove the convertible swiftly around the thread of road clinging to the edge of the island's cliffs. He said evenly, "My assistant told the housekeeper. I presume she let him know."

Holly was scandalized. "But it's rude!"

"Rude," he growled. "What about—"

Stavros cut himself off, staring stonily ahead at the sea.

"What about what?"

"Nothing."

"It's not like you to censor yourself."

"Forget it," he said abruptly. "Ancient history."

But he stomped on the gas, driving the red convertible faster along the cliff road of this small island in the Aegean.

Holly looked at him, from his tight shoulders to the grim set of his jaw. She said slowly, "Why haven't you spoken to your—"

Her voice cut off as they went past a grove of olive trees to a guarded gate. A white-haired guard approached the convertible, scowling. Then his eyes went wide. "Stavi?"

"Vassilis," he replied, smiling up at him. They spoke in Greek. Stavros indicated Holly and Freddie, mentioning their names. The guard replied, nearly jumping in his excitement, before he waved them through.

"You know him?" Holly said as Stavros drove the car past the gate.

"He was kind to me when I was young." His voice seemed strained. He roared the convertible up the hill, finally parking in front of a grand villa, whitewashed and sprawling across the cliff, on the edge of the sea. With a deep breath, Stavros abruptly turned off the engine. He stared up at the villa.

"Are you all right?" Holly asked.

He seemed almost as if he dreaded what was ahead. Which Holly didn't understand. What could there be to dread about a lavish villa on a Greek island paradise?

Unless it was the same thing that had made Stavros not speak to his father in twenty years. Holly suddenly wondered what they were getting into.

"Stavros," she said slowly, "I feel like there's something you're not telling me."

Without looking at her, he got out of the car. Unlatching the baby seat in the back seat of the convertible, Holly followed with Freddie.

They hadn't even reached the imposing front door of the villa before it flew open, revealing a plump, white-haired woman. She cried out, clasping her hands over her heart. "Stavi!"

Looking at her, his eyes went wide.

"Eleni?" he whispered.

Rushing forward, the petite, round woman threw her arms around him with a sob. She was much shorter than Stavros. Awkwardly, he patted her on the back. His expression was stricken. Holly couldn't look away from the raw emotion on his usually stoic face.

The white-haired woman spoke in rapid Greek, tears filling her eyes. He answered her slowly in the same language. She turned to the baby in Holly's arms.

Stavros said in English, "Holly, this is my father's housekeeper, Eleni. She's worked here since I was a child." Reaching out, he stroked his baby's soft dark head. "Eleni, this is my son, Freddie."

"Your son!" the housekeeper cried in accented English. She patted the baby's plump cheek with tears in her eyes. Eleni turned to Holly. "You are Stavros's wife?"

"Uh, no," Holly said awkwardly, shifting her baby's weight on her hip. "I'm Holly, his…" His what? Baby mama? Cast-off lover? "His, um, friend."

"Friend?" the housekeeper repeated with a frown.

Turning to Stavros, she said something sharply in Greek. Lips quirking, he answered her in the same language.

The old woman looked mollified. As servants collected their luggage and moved the convertible into the nearby garage, the housekeeper turned to Holly with an innocent smile. "You must be tired from your journey, Miss Holly, you and the baby. Everything is ready. Won't you come in, please?"

"Yes, thank you," Holly replied, throwing Stavros a confused glance as she followed them into the villa, cradling her baby in her arms.

Stavros's head tilted back as they walked through the foyer. "This place is smaller than I remember."

The housekeeper's wrinkled face smiled. "It is not smaller. You are bigger."

Small? Holly's eyes nearly popped out of her head as she looked around her. It was like a palace! The foyer opened directly into a huge room with a breathtaking view of the sun lowering into the sea with streaks of orange and red. An elegant chandelier hung high above the priceless antique furniture and marble floor.

Freddie gave a hungry whimper, and Eleni crooned, "Poor baby, you are tired. I will show you to your room."

Their room? As in, Holly and Stavros would be sharing one?

No. Surely not. Holly had made it very clear to Stavros that she had no interest in spending time with him. Especially not time of an intimate nature!

"Thank you, Eleni," Stavros said. He lifted a dark eyebrow. "When can I convince you to move to New York?"

"What would I do there? You live in a hotel!"

"Anything. Or nothing." He looked at her seriously. "You deserve to rest, after taking care of us when I was young. You were my mother's only friend when she was here. At least accept a pension?"

"Oh, no." Blushing, the older woman ducked her head. "I won't take charity."

"It's not charity. It's gratitude."

"No. I couldn't. But thank you, Stavi. If you ever need a housekeeper, let me know. You're a good boy." She smiled at him, then turned as servants passed with their luggage. "Your room is this way, if you please."

As they followed the housekeeper down a long

hallway, Holly whispered to Stavros, "What did you say to her earlier?"

He frowned. "When?"

Her cheeks went warm. "At the door when we arrived. When I said I was just your friend, she looked so upset. Until you said something to her in Greek."

"Oh." His black eyes gleamed with amusement. "I told Eleni not to worry. I will marry you soon."

His words caused a jolt that nearly made her trip. Then she rolled her eyes. "Funny."

Stavros raised an eyebrow. "You think I'm joking?"

He hadn't lost his arrogance, that was for sure. "I'll never marry you, Stavros. No way, no how."

He tilted his head with a crooked grin. "We'll see."

Holly's worst fears were confirmed when the housekeeper led them to a magnificent bedroom, with a balcony overlooking the sea. In the center of the room was a single enormous four-poster bed, and in the corner, a crib. Nearby, a changing table had been set up, with everything a baby could need. A rocking chair was placed by the windows.

"Perfect, yes?" Eleni said, smiling.

"It's beautiful, but…" Holly bit her lip as she looked around. "Where will I sleep?"

The housekeeper laughed, her eyes dancing. "I am not so old-fashioned as to believe you sleep in separate rooms." Going to the enormous walk-in closet, she said to Stavros, "For your wife and baby."

Just hearing herself described as Stavros's wife caused a frisson of emotion to dart through Holly. She stuck out her chin. "I'm not—"

"Thank you, Eleni," Stavros interrupted as he looked into the closet. Reaching into his pocket, he pulled out a stack of bills from his wallet. "Will this cover the cost of the clothes?"

Eleni shifted uncomfortably. "It's not necessary. Your father still owes you and your mother for what he never—"

"No," he said grimly. He gently placed the money in her hands. "You know I'd never take money from him."

"I know," the woman agreed. She looked at the bills. "But this is too much."

"Keep it." With a smile that didn't meet his eyes, he said, "You made my life here endurable. For Mom, too."

Hearing the strained edge to his voice, Holly stared at him. His face looked almost…vulnerable.

What had happened in his childhood? Why hadn't he spoken to his father in twenty years?

Not even the most gossipy secretaries in the New York office, the ones who kept track of Stavros's every lavish date with starlets and models, had spoken about his childhood. Stavros's American mother had died when he was a teenager. That was all they knew.

Now Holly felt like there was some big secret. Some tragedy. She watched as the petite, elderly woman hugged him fiercely, tears in her eyes, saying something in Greek.

Stavros stiffened, then shrugged, and said in English, "It's fine. I'm fine."

"It is good of you to bring the baby here to meet him," the housekeeper responded.

"Is he here?"

Eleni looked embarrassed. "Not yet. I did tell him about the baby. He knew you were coming." Her cheeks went red. "He said he might be back for dinner, but he might not, depending..."

"I remember how he was. With Mom."

The housekeeper looked sad, then squeezed his arm as she said softly, "Your mother was a good lady, Stavi. I was so sorry when I heard she died. I wish she could have lived to see all your success."

"Thank you." His handsome face held no expression. He pulled his arm away. "There is no point in waiting for him. Perhaps we could have dinner on the terrace?"

"Of course." Eleni brightened. "Whenever you like."

Stavros looked at Holly. "Are you hungry?"

As if on cue, her stomach growled noisily. She blushed as the others laughed. But dinner wasn't what she was worried about. She bit her lip. "Er, about this bedroom—"

"We'll have dinner in an hour," Stavros told the housekeeper, who nodded and left, still smiling.

Holly turned on him. "Stavros, you can't imagine we can share a bedroom!"

Stavros tilted his head, a half smile on his lips. "Can't I?" He glanced toward the baby, who'd started to fuss. "Freddie, what's wrong?" He reached out for the baby. "Let me—"

Instinctively, Holly moved the baby out of Stavros's reach. "He's tired."

He asked quietly, "I know I don't have experience. But won't you let me try to hold my son?"

It was the first time he'd asked.

"I'm sorry, it's not a good time." Holly's cheeks went hot. She, who always prided herself on being kind, knew she was being a jerk. She was just protecting Freddie, she told herself. It was only a matter of time before Stavros realized he didn't want to be a father. He would let them down. Why pretend otherwise? Why even let herself hope? "He's hungry. I need to give him a bath, then feed him and get him ready for bed."

"Of course," he said stiffly. Lowering his head, he tenderly kissed the baby's head. "Good night, my son."

Guilt built inside her, all the way to her throat.

He straightened, and said quietly to Holly, "Can you make your way to the terrace in an hour?"

"It's right outside that big room? By the foyer?"

He gave a short nod.

"I'll find it."

"Until then." With a small bow, he left. Holly looked after him, until the baby whimpered plaintively in her arms.

Was she being unkind, insisting on believing the worst of Stavros? Was it possible he actually wished to be a loving father to Freddie?

If he did, and Holly pushed him away from their son, then she would be the selfish one. Was she really protecting their baby? Or just wanting to punish Stavros, to make him suffer for the way he'd hurt her, by seducing and then abandoning her?

Lost in these unsettling thoughts, Holly gave her baby a bath in the en suite bathroom, then dried him off with a thick cotton towel. As she nuzzled his dark hair, breathing in his sweet newborn smell, she suddenly wished she'd never left Switzerland. All she wanted to do was be safe.

And nothing about Stavros Minos was safe. Not to her body. Not to her heart.

She shivered, remembering how his dark eyes had burned when he'd said he intended to marry her. Every moment she spent with him, every look, every innocent touch, reminded her of the night they'd conceived their child. Every moment close to him caused new sparks of need to crackle through her body.

She took a deep breath, looking out at the balcony where the sun was setting brilliantly over the Aegean Sea, past the palm trees. Oh, what she was doing on this remote Greek island, in a place that seemed expressly made for seduction?

Grabbing Freddie's old, clean footie pajamas from her overnight bag, she dressed him on the changing table and then carried him to the rocking chair near the window, overlooking the sea where the sun was falling into the water. Twenty minutes later, she tucked him into the crib, drowsy with a full belly.

Going to the en suite bathroom, Holly took a quick shower, avoiding her own eyes in the mirror. Wrapping herself in the thick white robe from the door, she went back into the closet and looked in her overnight bag. The thick hoodie, turtleneck and jeans she'd packed seemed all wrong for Greece. Snowy Switzerland seemed a million miles away.

Biting her lip, Holly slowly looked around the enormous closet. New clothes, in both her size and the baby's, had been neatly folded on the shelves and were hanging from the racks. Rising to her feet, she touched a white cotton sundress. For a moment, she was lost in a sudden dream, imagining soft fabric sliding over her skin as Stavros kissed her, his naked, powerful body hard against hers—

Electricity burned through her, making her breasts tighten and her body tremble.

No!

Holly couldn't allow herself to let down her guard. The last time she had, she'd ended up pregnant and alone.

And the stakes were far too high now. If she ever gave herself to Stavros again, either her body or her heart, he'd have the power to destroy her...and Freddie. She couldn't let that happen.

Holly lifted her chin. She was no longer an innocent girl who could be easily swayed by passionate kisses or sweet lies. She'd learned about consequences. She had a baby to think of.

This time, there was nothing Stavros could do to seduce her. If he truly wanted to help her raise their son, if his only intention was to be a good father, she would try to let him, for Freddie's sake.

She would have good manners. She would be courteous.

But Holly would never let Stavros back into her bed, or her heart. Never. Never ever!

Stavros stood out on the terrace, leaning against the white balustrade overlooking the cliff. He was still dressed in a tailored black button-down shirt and trousers that fit snugly against his body. He'd thought of changing to casual clothes, but there was no point in pretending to be casual, when the truth was, he felt anything but.

A table had been set up on the terrace, with

three place settings. But he knew his father would not come.

His jaw tightened, and he looked behind him at the house of his childhood. He felt his back break out in a cold sweat. How unhappy he'd been here. He still remembered his mother's wretchedness and heartbreak. His father hadn't just been selfish. He'd been cruel to her, flaunting his affairs, just to prove his power over her.

Now, the sprawling white villa glowed gold, orange and red, illuminated like King Midas's palace by the sun setting over the Aegean to the west.

It had been a shock to return here. He wondered how long he'd been frozen when he'd arrived in the convertible, staring up at the house. He'd been stunned to see Eleni. Like Vassilis, the guard, she'd grown much older. Even the villa, which had loomed so large in his youth, had grown much smaller. Or maybe, like Eleni had said, it was just Stavros who'd grown larger.

He'd lived here until he was eight. He had strong memories of his father's violent arguments with his mother, that had left Aristides shouting insults, and Rowena weeping. When, after years of emotional abuse, his mother could stand no more, she'd announced she was divorcing him and moving back to Boston.

In response, Aristides had coldly informed Stavros he could either remain in Greece as a rich man's son, or go to Boston to be a "nobody" and a "pitiful mama's boy."

Stavros had made his choice, and his father had been livid. He'd spoken with Aristides only once since then, when Stavros was seventeen. After months of ignoring his son's increasingly frantic phone messages, his father finally answered the phone on the day Stavros called to tell him Rowena had died.

"Why would I care about that?" Aristides had responded.

Now, every time Stavros thought of his mother's heartbreak, how hard she'd tried to love her husband through his betrayals, how hard she'd worked to try to support her child when the divorce had left her with nothing but custody of him…he was furious. His mother had died from overwork and grief, as much as the cancer that had claimed her life.

No wonder, when Stavros had gotten his own diagnosis, he'd been so sure he would obviously die. How could he live, when his mother—so much better and kinder than he—had not?

Setting his jaw, he stared out bleakly at the sea. The sun was setting, leaving a red trail against the dark water that looked almost like a trail of blood.

It was a strange irony that he had lived. And now he had a son of his own. He would not abandon Freddie. He wouldn't leave Holly to raise their son alone.

But how could he convince her to let him into their lives?

When Stavros had decided to bring her here from Switzerland, he'd been sure all he needed to do was spend a little time with her to make her see things his way.

But she'd shot him down every time he'd tried to speak with her on the jet. He didn't blame her. He was totally off his game. Being back in his childhood home had thrown him in ways he hadn't expected. Now, just when he most needed to be confident and powerful to win her, he was instead feeling uncomfortably vulnerable.

He hated it.

So how could he convince Holly? What could he do or say?

Sex wouldn't be enough. He'd felt the way she shivered when he "accidentally" touched her, seen the way she licked the corners of her mouth when he looked deeply into her eyes, as if waiting for his kiss. She wanted him.

But she didn't trust him. She refused to share a bedroom with him. Bedroom? Hell, she wouldn't even let him hold his son.

No mere charm, no regular seduction, would win her now. So what would?

Leaning against the balustrade, staring out at the sea, Stavros took a deep breath. Hearing a noise, he looked behind him.

And gasped.

Holly had come out on the terrace looking like a goddess of beauty, Aphrodite rising from the sea. She was wearing a simple white sundress, exposing her bare shoulders and legs to the pink light of the setting sun. Brilliant red hair tumbled over her shoulders like fire as she walked toward him in her sandals.

His heart lifted to his throat.

Coming close, she looked up at him, her green eyes big, her dark lashes trembling with emotion. "Good evening."

"Kaló apógevma," he replied. He held out his arm.

Ignoring it, she went straight to the table, without touching him.

Following her, he pulled out the chair. She sat

down, her lovely face expressionless. As he politely pushed the chair forward beneath the table, his fingers briefly brushed the soft bare skin of her back. He felt her tremble, which he'd expected.

But he trembled, too, which he hadn't.

Going to his own seat on the other side of the small table, he opened a waiting bottle. He paused. "Wine?"

"Just a taste."

He poured the white wine into two glasses, then passed one to her. His fingertips brushed hers, and again he felt her shiver. Again he held his breath.

Then she leaned back in her chair, looking away as she took a single sip of the wine, then placed it back quietly on the table.

No. Desire would not lure her this time.

Stavros lifted the silver lids off their china plates, and saw lamb and rosemary and potatoes. Sitting in the seat across from her, he sliced the lamb cleanly with his knife and chewed slowly. "You should try this. It's delicious." He smiled. "My favorite dinner from childhood. I can't believe Eleni remembered."

"She seems to think a lot of you."

"I think the same of her."

Holly ate almost mechanically, sipping mostly water, not meeting his eyes. He wondered what she was thinking about. Strange—he'd never had to wonder that about any woman before. Usually they couldn't wait to tell him. But Holly was different. Holly mattered—

Just that thought caused ice down his spine.

She mattered only because of his son. That was it. She'd never be more than the mother of his child to him. He'd never give her his heart. He couldn't, because he didn't have one.

The thought made him able to breathe again.

Biting her lip, Holly suddenly leaned forward. "I'm sorry about what you went through."

How did she know about his father's abandonment? Who had told her? He said stiffly, "What do you mean?"

Taking a deep breath, she said in a low voice, "I can't even imagine what you went through last year. Being sick. All alone."

"Oh." His shoulders relaxed. He was touched that she suddenly seemed to care. It gave him hope. "It's all right."

"No. It's not." Looking down at her hands, she said, "I just remember how I felt in the doctor's office when I found out I was pregnant." She looked up, her eyes glistening. "And that was happy news. I can't imagine going through what you did all alone. With no one at your side to help you through. To hold your hand."

A strange emotion rose inside him. Ruthlessly, he pushed it away. It was in the past. He'd battled through. He hadn't needed anyone then, and he didn't now. He was too strong for that. But he wanted to protect his child—and his child's mother.

Reaching over the table, he put his hand over her smaller one. His lips curved. "Does this mean you don't want me dead?"

An answering ghost of a smile touched her lips. "I never wanted you dead. I just…"

Her voice trailed off as she looked away.

The sun had disappeared, and the moon was rising in the darkening night. Stavros polished off his glass of wine, watching her. Wishing he could take her in his arms.

Looking up at the dark sky, Holly pulled her hand away. "The stars are bright here." She tilted back her head. "My dad and I used to look at the constellations together. He taught me a bunch of them. Orion." She pointed. "The Big Dipper, Gemini."

"He was an astronomer?"

She smiled. "A bus driver. Astronomy was his

hobby. A hobby he shared with my mother." Her smile lifted to a grin. "That made him want to learn even more about the stars to impress her. They used to go out driving at night, going outside the city to get away from the city lights. Until—"

Her expression changed and she looked down at her own still full wineglass.

"Until?"

"They went out on their twentieth wedding anniversary, and a drunk driver plowed into their car on the interstate."

"I'm sorry" was all he said, which seemed the wiser choice than "love always ends with tragedy."

"Don't be." She looked up, her eyes glistening. "My parents were happy, chasing their stars. My father always said loving my mother changed his life. She made him a husband. A father. More than he ever imagined he could be." She wiped her cheek with her shoulder. "He always said she changed his stars."

Her voice trembled with pride and love. And Stavros suddenly envied the man.

He poured another glass and took a gulp of wine. "You were lucky to have a father who loved you."

"You aren't close to yours."

Stavros barked a short laugh. "I despise him."

"You told me in Switzerland he was a good man."

"No, I said he was honest. It is not the same. He is honest about who he is. A greedy, selfish monster."

She stared at him, her face shocked.

"But perhaps you think the same about me." His lips twisted as he swished the wine in his glass. "That I am as selfish and coldhearted as every other man in my family." He looked up at the beautiful, tranquil villa. "I hate this place."

"This?" Holly looked up in bewilderment at the magnificent Greek villa, overlooking the dark Aegean Sea. She shook her head wryly. "You should have seen the house I grew up in. A two-bedroom apartment, with peeling wallpaper and a heater that broke down in winter."

"After my parents' divorce, my mother and I briefly lived in a homeless shelter in Boston."

He'd never shared that little tidbit with anyone. She looked shocked.

"How is that possible?" She pointed toward the villa. "There's no way you could be homeless. Not with a father as rich as that!"

"He cut my mother off without a penny in the divorce."

"How could he?"

"He found a way." A humorless smile traced his lips. "When my mother got tired of all his blatant cheating, he was too spiteful to even pay her the paltry amount guaranteed by the pre-nup. So he gave her a choice—if she voluntarily gave up that income, she could have full custody of me. He knew she'd agree." He took a drink. "The last thing she wanted was to leave me here with him."

"He cheated on your mother?"

Stavros snorted. "You think my cousin Oliver is bad? My father was worse. And my grand-father worse still. He impregnated every willing woman for miles around. My grandmother just gritted her teeth and pretended it wasn't hap-pening." He shook his head. "I don't even know all my cousins. Oliver's mother was the result of a fling between my grandfather and one of the maids."

"Oh," she said lamely.

Looking toward the sea, he said softly, "But my mother grew up in a different generation. She couldn't put up with it forever. Seeing her suffer broke my heart. I vowed I'd never be on either side of it."

"Never love anyone?"

"Or let them love me. Love always has a winner and a loser. A conqueror and a conquered." He gave a smile that didn't meet his eyes. "I decided long ago I never wanted to be either."

Holly looked past the villa's whitewashed terrace, illuminated by light from the villa behind them, to the black moon-swept sea beyond.

"But you still hurt me," she whispered. "In spite of that."

"I know." He took another slow, deliberate sip of wine. "No wonder when you found out you were pregnant, you decided I was a cruel bastard who didn't deserve either of you."

"Was I wrong?"

Her words seemed to echo in the soft Greek night. In the distance, he could hear the roar of waves pounding the beach.

"I was selfish when I seduced you," he said slowly. He lifted his gaze to hers. "But not when I let you go. I pushed you away because I was no good to anyone, least of all you."

"Like I said, you could have told me—"

"Holly, if I'd told you I was dying, it would have only bound you to me more. You would have given me everything, all your heart and your life, until I died—and even after. It would have destroyed you."

Her lovely face looked stricken, then angry.

"You really think I'm pathetic, don't you?" She raised her chin. "You're so sure I would have fallen in love with you?"

"Yes."

"Because you think you're irresistible." Her tone was a sneer that seemed like an ill-fitting costume on her.

Stavros took a deep breath. "Because you're the most loving person I've ever known. And I couldn't ruin your life like that." He gave a small smile. "Not even me."

Her eyes were huge and limpid in the moonlight.

"I expected to die," he continued in a low voice. "But to my surprise, I lived. And now we have a child. Surely you must see that my life can never be the same."

"It doesn't have to change for you…"

"You're wrong," he said simply. Reaching out, he took her hand across the table. "I want us to be a family."

He heard her breath catch. Her hand was suddenly trembling. Nervously, she tried to pull it away, turning toward the villa. "I should check on the baby..."

"Eleni will listen for him." He was close, so close, to achieving his objective. Leaning forward, holding her hand, he urged, "Give me a chance."

Silence fell. Then she said in a small voice, "It would take time for me to trust you again."

Joy rushed through him. "Whatever time you need—"

"I want separate bedrooms tonight."

Silence fell.

Separate bedrooms? That was not at all what he wanted. What he wanted was to make love to her tonight. Right now. But since he'd just promised her time, what else could he do?

"Very well," he said stiffly.

Exhaling, Holly looked out at the sea. "It's beautiful here. Like a dream." She tried to smile. "The white puffs of cloud look like ships in the moonlight."

Stavros watched her. "I like the joy you take in life. Most people forget that when they leave their childhoods behind. If they ever even knew."

She snorted, her expression incredulous. "You think I'm a child?"

"Far from it," he said quietly. "You're the most intensely desirable woman I've ever known."

Her eyes widened. Then her lips curled in a brief, humorless smile. She clearly didn't believe a word. "That's quite the compliment, considering how many you've known."

"None hold a candle to you." He looked at her across the table. "There's been no other woman for me, Holly. Not since we were together."

She blinked, then slowly looked at him. "What?"

"I don't want anyone else," he said simply.

For a moment, their eyes locked in the moonlight. He saw yearning in her lovely face. Then, as if on cue, the lights in the villa's windows behind them went dark, and she seemed to catch herself. Biting her lip, she rose with an awkward laugh. "It's late. I should go to bed."

Polishing off his glass of wine, he rose to his feet. "Of course."

"Should we bring in the plates?"

"It's not necessary."

"I don't want someone else cleaning up my mess." Picking up her plate and glass, she paused. "What about your father's plate?"

"Leave it." He added with irony, "He doesn't have your same concerns."

Stavros picked up his own plate and glass, and the bottle of wine. As they walked back across the terrace, he felt the chill of the deepening night. A cool sea breeze blew against his skin. He looked up at the sprawling white villa.

Getting her into bed was going to take longer than he'd thought. And marrying her would be even longer.

But he didn't know how much more of his past he could share with her. Every small story was like pulling his soul through a meat slicer. He would have far preferred to seduce her.

But he'd seen the change in her. He saw it now, as they took the dishes back to the enormous, modern kitchen. The anger in her eyes when she looked at him had changed to bewilderment, even wistfulness. His plan was working.

So he'd just have to endure it.

Stavros walked her back to their large guest bedroom. Passing her without a word, he quickly grabbed his leather overnight bag. He paused only to look down at his baby, sleeping in the crib. He didn't touch him, out of fear he might wake.

"Good night, my son," he whispered.

Freddie yawned, his eyes closed as he continued to sleep, flinging his chubby arms back over his head.

Stavros turned, lifted his bag over his shoulder and started down the hall. Turning back to say good-night, he stopped when he saw Holly standing in the doorway. Her heart-shaped face was haunted.

"Do you really care about Freddie?" she said hoarsely. "You're not just doing it out of pride, or to hurt me? You really want to be his father?"

"Yes," he said in a low voice. He dropped the bag to the floor and moved close to her. "And I want you."

She looked up, her expression stricken. "You..."

"I want you. I want to hold you in my arms. I want you in my bed. I've tried to forget that night. I can't. I've thought of it for the last year."

She trembled, searching his gaze.

"You're trying to seduce me," she whispered.

"Yes. I am." Cupping her face, he lowered his head toward hers. "I want you forever..."

And in the shadowy hall outside the bedroom, he lowered his lips toward hers and kissed her, soft and slow.

For a moment, she froze beneath his embrace, and he thought she'd push him away.

Then slowly, tremblingly, her lips parted. And

it was the sweetest, purest kiss Stavros had ever known. It took every ounce of his willpower to finally pull away, when all he wanted to do was take her back into the bedroom and make love to her.

But he didn't want her for just one night. He wanted her as his wife. And if he'd learned anything from nearly twenty years in mergers and acquisitions, it was to always leave the other side wanting more.

"Good night," he said huskily, cupping her cheek as he looked deeply into her eyes. And he left her.

CHAPTER EIGHT

HOLLY HAD TOSSED and turned all night in the big bed.

She couldn't stop thinking of Stavros's voice last night.

Holly, if I'd told you I was dying it would have only bound you to me more. You would have given me everything, all your heart and your life, until I died—and even after. It would have destroyed you.

Put that way, she could almost forgive him for what he'd done. Because he was right. If, last Christmas, he'd taken her in his arms and told her the truth, she would have immediately done anything, given anything, to help him.

You're the most loving person I've ever known.

He'd made it sound like a character flaw.

Maybe it was. She thought of how she'd spent all her adult life caring for others over herself. She didn't mean Freddie. He was a helpless baby. But Oliver wasn't helpless. Neither was her sister. And for years, Holly had sacrificed herself for their needs, for no good reason. She thought of how Nicole had blamed Holly on the phone for their marriage problems.

You should be here taking care of things for him. And for me!

Maybe Stavros was right. Maybe, in some ways, Holly's need to always put other people first had been wrong. It certainly hadn't done anything good for Nicole or Oliver, who only seemed more helpless and resentful after her years of sacrifice.

And if Holly had let herself fall in love with Stavros last year, she suddenly knew she would have given him everything, too—whether he wanted it or not.

Instead, when he'd rejected her, she'd been forced to do everything on her own. She'd gained strength, and confidence she'd never had before. Both important qualities for a good mother.

And for a good father?

She shivered. She was starting to believe that Stavros really cared about Freddie, and wanted to be a family. He seemed determined to marry Holly.

Could they actually be happy together?

The idea was growing harder to resist. It would

be too easy to love a man like Stavros, when he poured on the charm. She fell a little every time he spoke to her. And when he'd kissed her—

All night afterward, she'd lain awake, wondering what would have happened if she hadn't insisted on separate bedrooms. If she'd let him share her bed. Wondering, and knowing. And wishing...

Now, as Holly looked at Stavros across the breakfast table, with the morning sun shining gold from the double-story window and the sea outside a brilliant blue, her heart was in her throat.

They barely said a word to each other as they ate breakfast. She was dressed simply, in a T-shirt and jeans, while he was in his usual tailored shirt, jacket and trousers. He'd just looked at her, then kissed her on the cheek. But that had been enough to make her pulse pound.

"I know what you're thinking," Stavros said now as his eyes met hers over the table. She broke out in a hot sweat.

"Oh?" she said, praying he didn't.

He tilted his head. "You're wondering how long we have to wait. I say we don't."

"Really?" she croaked, still filled with images of him naked in her bed.

He gave her a crooked grin. "Honestly, I'm glad my father never showed up last night. I only brought you here because I couldn't think of any other way to convince you to give me a chance. I knew with your loving heart, you would feel like you had no choice but to let him meet his grandson."

Her *loving heart* really was starting to sound ridiculous. As if Holly was determined to see only the best in people, even when her positive image of them was totally untethered to reality. What she'd learned last night about Stavros's father didn't make her particularly keen to get to know him better, either.

As Freddie started fussing in her arms, she reached for a prepared bottle on the table. "You want to leave after breakfast? Without seeing him?"

"It would feel like dodging a bullet." Leaning forward, he suddenly asked, "Could I hold the baby, Holly?"

His darkly handsome face was vulnerable, his deep voice uncertain, as if he wasn't just asking her permission, but her opinion.

He still hadn't held their son yet. Because Holly hadn't let him.

Suddenly, she hated herself for that. Who did

she think she was, keeping Freddie from Stavros—a man who'd made it clear that he only wanted good things for their baby?

"Of course you can," she said. "You're his father."

His dark eyes lit up. "Yes?"

"Definitely." Gently, she lifted the two-month-old into his father's strong arms, where Stavros sat on the other side of the breakfast table in the morning room. She handed him a warmed bottle. "You'll need this."

"Like this?" he asked, angling the bottle. His boyish uncertainty made her heart twist inside her.

"Tilt your elbow a little more," she suggested, touching his bare forearm. He looked up at her, and for a moment, electricity crackled between them. She saw him start to rise, as if he intended to take her in his arms.

Then he looked back down at the baby, and didn't move from his chair. Freddie wrapped his hands around the bottle, drinking with greedy gulps, his black eyes looking up at his father trustingly.

Holly watched them with a lump in her throat. The baby's sucking noises gradually slowed, then stopped altogether, as his eyes grew drowsy as he drifted off to sleep, held tenderly in his father's powerful arms.

Stavros looked up with obvious pride, his dark eyes shining.

"Look," he whispered. "He's sleeping!"

And something broke inside Holly's heart.

Stavros seemed so different now—

"So you finally came crawling back."

Holly looked up to see a wiry, elderly man standing in the doorway with two young women on his arm. The man had brightly colored, youthful clothes that did little to disguise his potbelly and skinny legs. His hair was pitch-black, except for half an inch near the roots that was white. Even from this distance, he reeked of alcohol, cigarettes and expensive cologne.

Stavros's face turned briefly pale. As if by instinct, he turned his body in the chair, as if protecting the sleeping baby. Then, as if a wall came clanging down, his expression became totally flat.

"Hello, Father." His bored gaze glanced dismissively at the two young women, both of whom looked younger than Holly, perhaps even younger than her little sister. "Friends of yours?"

"From the club." He waved toward them airily.

"We stopped to change clothes. Or at least—" he gave a sly grin "—take them off."

Holly looked with dismay at the girls, who both looked, if possible, even more bored than Stavros. They had to be a third of Aristides's age. One of them was already giving Stavros a frankly flirtatious smile that made Holly, who'd never considered herself prone to violence, want to give her a hard smack across the jaw.

The older man stepped forward, then looked down at the sleeping baby with a sniff. "Is that the baby Eleni was going on about?"

"This is my son, yes," Stavros said stiffly.

"Looks tiny. Runt of the litter."

"He's two months old."

Aristides winked back at the young women. "I'm sure you girls can hardly believe I'm old enough to be a grandfather."

"Uh, yeah," the blonde replied with an American accent, turning so that her friend could see her roll her eyes. "Look, Aristi, if we're not going out shopping like you promised then we've got to go."

"Things to see, people to do," her brunette friend agreed, giving Stavros another flirtatious smile.

"No, wait—I have gifts for you girls upstairs. Go up and wait."

"Where?"

"Up the top of the stairs. The big purple bedroom all the way at the back," he called jovially, then ran his hands slickly through his hair. After they were gone, he turned on Stavros with a scowl. "So why did you come here?"

"No reason."

"You want money, right?"

Stavros stiffened. "No."

Aristides stared at him, then shrugged. "All right, fine, I saw the kid. Now get the hell out of here. You're nothing to me. I have no desire to be a grandfather."

Holly could hardly believe it. She tried to imagine a world in which she'd ever ignore family, or tell a son or grandson that he wasn't wanted. The thought was like an ice pick in her heart.

"Are you serious?" she blurted out. "After we came all this way?"

Aristides's rheumy, drunken eyes focused on her. "Who are you? The wife?"

"She's my son's mother." Stavros's voice was low. Holly felt, in her bones, how much he would have liked to claim her as his wife.

"Ha! So not your wife. She had your kid, but you still didn't marry her?" The man snorted a laugh. "Maybe you learned from my mistakes after all. You're more like me than I thought, boy."

"I'm nothing like you," Stavros growled, his hands tightening around his sleeping baby son.

"No?" His father stroked his chin. "You were so high and mighty when you called me after your mother's funeral. I was a monster, you said. You'd never whore around like me, you said. Now look at you."

Stavros looked speechless with rage.

Turning to Holly with a crafty expression, Aristides purred, "You're smart not to marry him. What did you say your name was?" Without waiting for her to answer, he continued flirtatiously, "A beauty like you can do far better."

With a sly glance toward his son, Aristides Minos lifted a calculating eyebrow, as if plotting what to say next; for an appalling instant Holly wondered if he was considering inviting her to join the other girls in his bedroom. Suddenly, she couldn't stand it.

"I didn't want to have a wedding while I was pregnant. But Stavros and I are getting married soon," Holly said, meeting the older man's gaze steadily. "In a few days."

She felt, rather than heard, Stavros's intake of breath.

"Your loss," Aristides said, sounding bored. "All right. Thanks for the visit." He looked down at his son scornfully. "But don't think that this means I'll put you back in my will."

"Are you kidding?" Holly said, outraged. "Do you actually think he needs your money?"

"Shh, Holly. It doesn't matter." Holding his sleeping baby carefully, Stavros rose to his feet. He was taller than his father, and his expression was utterly cold. "Keep your money, you cheap bastard."

"Cheap!" The older man's eyes blazed. "Just because I wasn't willing to hand off my family fortune to some little waitress I met in a bar, who convinced me to marry her when she got pregnant." He scowled at Stavros. "I'm still not sure you're even mine."

"I wish to hell I wasn't," he said quietly.

"Gotten full of yourself with that company of yours? Just because you think you're richer than me now?" His father drew himself up, slicking his hand back through his skunk-striped hair. "You'd never have built that company without me."

Stavros's eyes went wide. "You say that, after what you did to Mom—"

"If I hadn't cut her off without a penny, you'd never have had the drive to make something of yourself. You should thank me." Aristides tilted his head, in the exact same gesture she'd seen Stavros use. "I should own half your stock, purely as an issue of fairness."

Stavros's fists tightened, then he looked at his baby sleeping nestled in the crook of one arm, and he exhaled.

"You're not worth another minute of my time," he said, and he turned to Holly. "Are you ready?"

"Definitely."

"Good. Go!" His father's black eyes narrowed as his voice built in rage. "Get out of my house!"

Holly looked for one last moment at the rich, horrible old man. "Goodbye. Sorry you've made such bad choices in life."

Aristides looked shocked.

Without another word, Holly turned and followed Stavros out of the villa's morning room.

"I'm sorry, too!" he screamed after her. "Sorry I wasted my time talking to you! You're not even that pretty!"

She expected Stavros to head upstairs to get

their overnight bags, but instead he went straight for the front door, pausing only to talk to Eleni, the housekeeper.

Following him outside, Holly said quietly, "What about our things?"

"We'll get new ones. I'm done here."

"I understand."

"Eleni's gone to pack. She heard everything and says she can't work for him anymore." Stavros lifted a phone to his ear and spoke to his pilot. She saw how his hand trembled as he ended the call. Turning to her, he said quietly, "Did you mean what you said?"

Holly couldn't pretend not to know what he meant.

"Yes." She looked down at their precious sleeping baby cradled against his chest. "I want us to be a family." She lifted her gaze to his and whispered, "I'll marry you."

His dark gaze filled with light. "You'll come to New York?"

With a deep breath, she nodded. He cupped her cheek, running his thumb along her tender bottom lip, causing electricity to pulse through her body.

"You won't be sorry," he promised.

Shivering, Holly prayed he was right.

* * *

New York City was a winter wonderland, decorated with fresh snow and all the lights and decorations of Christmas. To Stavros, the city had never looked so beautiful. It was as if all the world had decided to celebrate.

Today was his wedding day.

His wife. Holly was going to be his wife…

Since their arrival from Greece, their wedding plans had been rushed through in only two days. Stavros wished to marry her as quickly as possible, before she had the chance for second thoughts.

Also, he had a major upcoming business deal, the acquisition of a local technology business-management firm for nearly two billion dollars, which he knew would keep him busy the last weeks before Christmas.

And as in all acquisitions, Stavros had learned from experience that speed was key. Once a man knew what he wanted, there was nothing to be gained from waiting. Better to strike fast, and possess what he wanted, before anyone else could take it. That was true in business—and marriage.

Holly had agreed to be married as soon as they could get the license. Her only request was that they invite her sister to the wedding. Apparently when she'd phoned Nicole with the news, her little sister had begged to bring Oliver to the ceremony, too. Stavros was none too pleased. He cynically expected his cousin, who'd been unemployed for months, to ask him for money. But having her sister there seemed important to Holly's happiness, and her happiness was important to his.

When Holly had said she'd marry him, Stavros thought he would explode with joy.

No, not joy, he told himself. Triumph. He'd achieved his objective. His son was secure. Or he would be, as soon as they were married today. They'd be a family. And Holly would be in his bed.

Stavros pictured how she'd looked in the moonlight, so unabashedly emotional. She didn't seem to realize how foolish it could be, to show feelings, to even have them at all: it left you vulnerable. He felt uncomfortable remembering everything he'd shared with her in Greece. He'd never been that open with anyone.

He'd only done it to achieve his objective, he reassured himself. There was no danger of him giving his heart to Holly, no matter how tempted any other man would be. Stavros's heart had been charred to ash long ago.

He'd meant it when he'd told her she'd never regret marrying him. But he'd have to walk a careful line. He wanted to make her happy, but not so happy she fell in love with him. He couldn't be that cruel, when he'd never be able to return her love. And he couldn't bear the thought of hurting her. Dread went through Stavros at the thought.

He remembered how she'd spoken so dreamily about how her parents had loved each other.

My father always said loving my mother changed his life. She made him a husband. A father. More than he ever imagined he could be. He always said she changed his stars.

Holly knew that love wasn't something that Stavros—or any Minos man—was capable of, he told himself firmly. She'd still chosen to marry him. Therefore, she'd accepted him as he was.

He might not be able to experience love, or give it, but damn it, he'd be faithful to her. He'd be a solid husband and father. He'd always provide for her and the baby.

He'd made sure of that in their prenuptial agreement, much to the dismay of his lawyers.

His terms had been far more generous than needed. But he wanted Holly to know she'd never be left penniless by a divorce, as his own mother had.

If he couldn't love Holly, he'd make damn sure she was always cared for.

Stavros could hardly wait to make her his wife and make love to her. It was all he'd been able to think of on the flight from Greece. He would have taken Holly back to the jet's bedroom while the baby slept, if it hadn't been for the presence of Eleni. Nothing like a sharp-eyed, grandmotherly former nanny aboard to keep one's basest desires in check.

A judge would be arriving later today to marry them at his penthouse, which was already decorated with candles, flowers and Christmas holly and ivy. The rings had been bought, the wedding dress and tuxedo secured and the food arranged by the wedding planner.

Somewhat to his shock, Holly had let the planner sort out everything.

"You don't even want to pick out your dress?" Stavros had grinned. "You are the most easygoing bride in the world."

She'd shrugged. "It doesn't really matter."

He'd sobered. "Are you sure? If a big wedding

is important to you, Holly, we can be married in a cathedral and invite the whole damn city."

She shook her head. "I had my dream wedding last year, for Nicole. And I'm not sure it made any difference for them." She lifted her gaze to his and said, "Our marriage is what I care about, not the ceremony."

Cradling her head in his hands, he gently kissed her. "But you deserve a party..."

She'd looked at him for a long moment. "I'd rather have this day just be about us. But if you really want to throw me a party, you know what I'd really like? A birthday party on the twenty-third of December, with all my friends."

"The twenty-third?" He was ambushed by the memory of that date last year, when he'd gotten his fatal diagnosis.

She'd smiled. "It's why my parents named me Holly, because my birthday's so close to Christmas." She tilted her head. "For just one time, I'd love to have a real birthday party, without Christmas taking over..."

Then she happily told him a story he barely heard, something about everyone always wrapping her birthday gifts in Christmas paper, or giving her a single gift for a combined Christmas/birthday present, or forgetting her birthday entirely. But he was distracted by memories of the shock and weakness and vulnerability he'd felt last year. He never wanted to feel like that again.

Especially now. As a father, soon to be a husband, he couldn't afford to ever feel weak or vulnerable again. He wasn't afraid of the cancer returning. His recent checkup had placed him in full remission. But emotionally, he'd have to be strong to make sure he never totally let down his walls. He didn't want to hurt Holly. Or be hurt himself…

"Of course." As she finished her story, Stavros gave her a charming smile. "The best birthday party you've ever seen."

Then they went to city hall, where a very bored-looking city employee gave them a marriage license, and an excited paparazzo took their picture as they left.

Within twenty minutes of the photo getting posted online, he'd started getting phone calls from shocked acquaintances and ex-girlfriends around the world, demanding to know if it was true and the uncatchable playboy was actually getting married. He'd ignored the messages. Why explain? Silence was strength.

But now that Stavros was about to speak his

wedding vows, he felt oddly nervous. He'd told himself that he was different from the other Minos men. He was determined to be an excellent husband and father. But what if he was wrong? What if he broke Holly's heart?

He'd make sure it didn't happen. If he cared for her, respected her, honored and provided for her, how could it matter if he loved her or not? How would she even know the difference?

Stavros was distracted by a hard knock at his penthouse bedroom door. Turning, he saw his cousin, who'd arrived with Nicole an hour before, looking shifty-eyed in his well-cut tuxedo.

"I say, old man," Oliver said with an artificially bright smile. "Before you speak vows and all that, I wonder if I could have a word?"

Stavros checked his expensive platinum watch.

"I have five minutes," he said shortly.

He'd regretfully agreed to Holly's suggestion that his cousin could be best man, as Nicole had begged her to be matron of honor. It made sense, the two of them returning the favor after Stavros and Holly had done it for them the previous year.

But Stavros and his cousin had never been particularly close, and Oliver had been a very unsatisfying employee at his company. And since the other couple's awkward arrival at the penthouse, Oliver had seemed to be working up to something. Stavros had a good idea what it was. He set his jaw.

"You might have heard," Oliver began, "that I've rather had trouble finding work…"

"Because your employers actually expect you to work?"

His cousin gave a crooked grin. "Turns out I'm not good at it."

"Or interested in it." Checking that he had the wedding ring in his pocket, Stavros looked at himself one last time in the full-length mirror and adjusted his tuxedo tie. "So?"

"I never thought you'd get married, Stavros. I always figured I'd be your heir."

"Sorry to disappoint you." Since he was only a few years older than Oliver, it was a little disconcerting to realize his cousin had counted on his death as a retirement plan.

Oliver paused. "It's funny to see you in love. I never thought you'd fall so hard for any woman."

Stavros didn't bother to disabuse him of the notion he was in love with his bride. It seemed like bad form on their wedding day. "What did you want to ask me?"

"Right. Well. Since it's obvious how much Holly's happiness means to you…" Oliver gave his most charming grin. "I wonder if you'd be willing to pay me ten million dollars to stay married to Holly's sister."

CHAPTER NINE

"COME ON, HOLLY. Please! You have to help me!"

Her little sister's insistent, whining voice hurt Holly's ears as she sat in the chair of the penthouse's guest bedroom, waiting for the stylists to finish doing her hair and makeup for her wedding.

When Nicole had begged to be her matron of honor, Holly had actually hoped it was because she wanted them to be close again. Instead, she'd spent the last twenty minutes blaming Holly for her marriage problems and asking for money.

"I'm sorry, Nicole. I can't just tell Stavros to hire Oliver back." She hesitated. "We both know he wasn't a very good employee…"

"Oh, so you don't care if my marriage is ruined? If we both starve? How can you be so unfeeling? You're my sister!"

Holly's cheeks were hot as she glanced at the two stylists, who were pretending not to listen. "Fine," she sighed. "I have five thousand dollars in my retirement account. It will be a little hard to get it out but if you really need it—"

"Five thousand dollars? Are you out of your mind?" Nicole cried. "That's nothing! My handbags cost more than that!"

The two stylists glanced at each other. Holly's cheeks burned even hotter. She asked the makeup artist, "Am I done?"

"Yes." The woman put final touches on her lips. "Now you are."

"Thank you." She looked around for her bag. "I'll get my wallet—"

"We've already been paid by your husband," the stylist said, smiling at her. "And lavishly tipped, I might add."

"Congratulations, Mrs. Minos," the other stylist said warmly. "I hope you will be very happy."

Mrs. Minos. Just the name caused a flutter inside Holly's belly. As the stylists gathered their equipment and disappeared, she looked at herself. She hardly recognized the glamorous bride in the mirror, with her glamorous makeup and unruly red hair tamed into an elegant chignon beneath a veil.

She was wearing expensive lingerie, a strapless bustier and white panties, and a white garter holding up old-fashioned white stockings.

The long, translucent veil stretched behind her. For a moment, she was lost in a dream, picturing a lifetime as Stavros's wife, the two of them in love forever—

In love? Where had that idea come from?

"It's easy for you to be happy," Nicole said resentfully. "With all your money." Lifting Freddie, who was whining in a similar tone, from his nearby crib, she said to the baby, "You're the luckiest kid in the world."

Lifting her simple white wedding dress from where it was spread over the bedspread of the guest bed, Holly said distractedly, "You don't believe that, Nicole. You know it's not money that makes a happy home, but love. And your money problems will work themselves out. You have a college degree. You could always look for a job yourself…"

"It's not just money." Cuddling her nephew close, Nicole closed her eyes. She took a deep breath. "Oliver's cheating on me, Holly."

Holly stiffened as she held her simple strapless white dress over her undergarments. "Oh, no!"

"He only married me because I threatened to break up with him if he didn't. But that was when he had an easy job and plenty of money.

Now, he regrets he ever married me. I'm not good enough."

"That's ridiculous!" Scowling, she whirled to face her little sister. "He's the one who's not remotely good enough—"

"He's going to leave me for someone rich," she choked out, wiping her eyes. "I just know it. And I'll be all alone."

When she saw Nicole's woebegone face, Holly's heart broke for her.

"It'll be all right, Nicky," she whispered, using her old childhood nickname as she reached out to touch her shoulder. "Everything's going to be all right."

"I'm so sorry." Trying to smile, Nicole choked back her tears. "I'm wrecking your wedding day. We can talk about this all later."

But as Holly left the guest bedroom a few minutes later, and went into the grand salon of the penthouse, she still felt troubled. And not just by what she'd learned from her sister, who was dressed in a pink bridesmaid's dress, following her with yawning Freddie, resplendent in a baby tuxedo.

Holly's teeth chattered nervously as she thought of the irrevocable vows she was about to take. Just this time last year, she'd been planning

Nicole's wedding. She'd never expected she'd so soon be a bride herself. Now, as she walked down the short hallway, she clutched her simple bouquet of pink peonies as if her life depended on it.

She was getting married.

To him.

Stavros stood waiting near the Christmas tree, imposing and breathtakingly handsome in front of the floor-to-ceiling windows with all of New York City at his feet. Next to him stood Oliver, blond and debonair. On his other side was the jocular, white-haired judge who would marry them, smiling broadly in his black robes, and lastly Eleni, in an old-fashioned, formal dress, beaming as if she herself were mother of the groom.

But Holly had eyes only for Stavros.

He was wearing a sleek tuxedo that clung to his powerful, muscular body. Her eyes moved up from his black tie to his powerful neck, his square jaw, his gorgeous face. His dark eyes burned through her.

Their wedding ceremony was simple, lasting only a few minutes. It seemed like a dream.

She couldn't look away from his face.

"And do you, Holly Ann Marlowe, take this man to be your lawfully wedded husband…?"

"I do," she breathed, trembling as he slid the huge diamond ring over her finger.

"And do you, Stavros Minos, take this woman to be your lawfully wedded wife?"

"I do," he growled in his low, sexy voice, looking at her in a way that made her toes curl in her high-heeled shoes. And suddenly, all her nervousness about the permanency of their wedding vows melted away.

"Then by the power vested in me by the State of New York, I now pronounce you husband and wife." The judge beamed between them. "You may now kiss the bride."

Stavros's dark, hooded eyes held the red spark of desire as he took her in his arms. As he lowered his lips to hers, her breasts felt heavy, her nipples taut beneath the sweetheart neckline of the silk wedding dress. Tension coiled low and deep in her belly.

For days, he'd been teasing her with butterfly kisses and little touches. Now, his kiss made her forget all her doubts and regrets. It made her forget her own name.

Then she remembered: her name had changed.

From this moment forward, she was Mrs. Holly Minos.

She watched the judge sign the marriage license, followed by Nicole and Oliver, as witnesses. She saw Nicole look at her husband nervously, with pleading in her eyes. Oliver gave his wife a warm smile, put his arm around her and kissed her forehead. Nicole looked as if she was about to cry with relief.

Holly exhaled. Her sister must have been wrong. Oliver couldn't be cheating on her, not if he kissed her like that. Everything would be fine...

"Congratulations, you two," the judge said, smiling at Holly and Stavros. "Now I'll leave you—" he winked "—to your private celebrations."

Holly's eyes went wide. *Private celebrations.* She looked up at the handsome, powerful man beside her. *Her husband.*

She'd only had one lover her whole life, and for only one night. She'd never forgotten the way Stavros had made her feel so alive, or the ecstasy of his touch. The night she'd spent with him last Christmas Eve had been the most magical of her life, before it had all come crashing down the next morning.

But there would be no more rejection. They were married now. For better, for worse. For the rest of their lives…

"We'll head downstairs," Eleni said happily, holding Freddie, who looked very sleepy in his baby tuxedo. Stavros had hired Eleni as their highly paid part-time housekeeper. Holly wasn't sure it was necessary, but how could she object to Stavros giving a job to the woman who'd taken care of him in childhood?

Besides, she liked and trusted Eleni, and was grateful the other woman would be watching Freddie tonight in her new suite downstairs, giving them privacy for their wedding night.

Holly shivered. *Their wedding night.*

"We'll go now, too," Nicole said, leaning back against her husband, who cuddled her close.

"Talk later?" Holly said to her anxiously, thinking of their earlier discussion. Her little sister smiled.

"Stop worrying," she said cheerfully, patting her on the shoulder. "You need to be more selfish. You're a bride."

And everyone left at once. For the first time since Freddie had been born, Holly was alone.

Alone with her husband…

"Mrs. Minos," Stavros murmured. He slowly

looked her over, making her shiver inside. Then, without a word, he lifted her up in his arms, against his chest. He looked down at her. "I've waited a long time for this night."

"Days," she sighed, thinking of the anticipation she'd felt since they'd left Greece.

Stavros looked at her seriously. "A year."

He carried her down the penthouse hall, then set her down gently beside the same enormous bed where, last Christmas Eve, they'd conceived their son. She glanced down at it, thinking how much had changed since then.

They had a future. They were a family.

Gently, he pulled off the headband of white silk flowers that held her long veil in place. He dropped it on the nightstand.

The gas fire caused flickers of white light to move against the dark shadows of his face. The room was black, gray and white. The Christmas tree lights. Through the windows, New York City at night.

Taking off his tuxedo jacket, he dropped it silently to the floor, along with his black tie. He unbuttoned the cuffs of his shirt. Never taking his gaze off hers, he reached his powerful arms around her and unzipped her strapless wedding gown. It slid down her body to the floor, revealing her white bustier bra, tiny white lace panties and white garter.

She heard the low shudder of his breath, felt the tremble of his hands as he stepped back to look at her.

"You're magnificent," he whispered.

The heat in his gaze melted her. All she could think about was that she wanted to make him hers. *Forever.*

Reaching forward, Holly yanked on his white shirt, popping off buttons that scattered to the floor. She could hardly believe her own boldness as she reached inside his open shirt to slowly stroke down his hard-muscled bare chest, lightly dusted with dark hair.

With a low growl, he grabbed her wrists. For a moment, he just looked down at her, his black eyes searing her. Then without a word, he pushed her back on the bed.

Never taking his gaze off her, her husband took off his shirt, dropping it the floor. She had the sharp image of his powerful bare chest, all shadows and hollows in the flickering firelight. She reached toward him. She couldn't wait. She had to feel his body, his weight. She had to feel him against her. *Now.*

"Stavros," she whispered, arms extended.

He moved instantly, climbing over her on the bed in a single athletic movement. She exhaled as she felt his body over hers, his heavy weight pushing her into the mattress, felt the bare skin of his chest and arms against hers. Lifting himself up on one powerful arm, he cupped her cheek, looking down at her intently.

"You're mine now," he whispered. "And I'm never going to let you go…"

He lowered his lips to hers, softly at first. Then his embrace deepened, turning hungry, almost savage. Her nipples tightened beneath her white silk bustier as his powerful muscles moved against her. As he kissed her, he stroked down her cheek, her neck, her shoulder. He cupped her breast over the silk, then reached beneath it to caress her taut nipple, making her gasp.

Pulling away, he looked down at her, his eyes dark. Sitting up, he pulled the silk off her body as if it was nothing more than a thought. Lowering his head between her full breasts, he kissed down the valley between them, all the way to the soft curve of her belly. He ran his hands over the edge of her hips, where her white lace panties clung, digging into her skin. He kissed her belly button, flicking his tongue inside it, as he unbuckled her garters. His large hands caressed each cheek of her bottom before he slowly moved down her body. Sensually, he rolled down each white stocking, soft as a whisper and elusive as a dream.

As the silk slid slowly down her skin, he followed it with kisses down one leg, then the other, down her thighs to the curve beneath her knees, all the way to the hollows of her feet. She shivered on the bed, feeling vulnerable, wearing only her tiny thong panties. After tossing the stockings aside, he pushed her legs apart. She looked up at him in the silver-white firelight, which left dancing patterns across his powerful naked chest.

She looked at his trousers, then met his eyes as she whispered like a fearless wanton woman, "Take them off."

He moved so rapidly he was almost a blur, ripping off his trousers and the dark boxers beneath. In half a second, they were on the floor, and he was on her.

Then her flimsy lace panties were gone, disintegrated beneath the force of his powerful hands. Cupping her breasts, he positioned himself between her legs. As he lowered his head, possessing her lips with his own, she felt the hard thickness of him pressing between her thighs.

Her hips moved of their own volition, swaying against him, as her hands raked down his back, settling against his hard-muscled backside.

She felt his powerful body shiver. Lifting his head, he looked down at her face. For a moment, she thought he would say something, something that could either annihilate her or make her soul explode with joy—one or the other. Instead, he just lowered his head and kissed her fiercely. Pulling his hips back, he thrust inside her in a single smooth movement, making her gasp as he filled her, all the way to the hilt.

Her fingernails dug into his skin as she looked up at his handsome face. His eyes were closed, his expression one of ecstasy.

Drawing back, he pushed inside her a second time, this time very slowly, so she could feel him, inch by inch. She closed her own eyes, surrendering to the pleasure building inside her, spiraling rapidly out of control.

She gasped as he suddenly moved, rolling her on top of him. Her eyes flew open. She looked down at him.

He reached up and tenderly caressed her cheek.

"I want to watch you," he whispered. His hands moved down the edge of her throat, lazily cupping her full breast, stroking his thumb against her taut, aching nipple. "I want to see what your face is like when you're the one in control."

Stavros looked up at his bride, naked astride him on the enormous bed in his penthouse bedroom.

He was telling her the truth. But not all of it. He watched the play of lights and shadows on her beautiful face. Across the room, the artificial Christmas tree sparkled in front of floor-to-ceiling windows revealing Manhattan at their feet.

He did want to see her in control. But only because, being inside her, he'd been about to lose his own.

She felt too good. She felt too tight. After a year of rampant hunger, of repressed longing, he'd nearly lost his mind pushing inside her once. For the second thrust, he'd applied the brakes, going as slowly as possible. But that hadn't helped. He'd known, if he thrust a third time, that he would have exploded inside her.

Hardly the wedding night he wanted, or the one Holly deserved. And so he'd rolled on his back, thinking to give his willpower some respite. If she controlled the rhythm, surely he could make it last.

Instead, as he looked up now into her glowing emerald eyes, he saw the red blush on her cheeks as she bit down harder on her swollen lower lip, and his shaft, already so hard he groaned with need, flexed instinctively. She hesitated, glancing down at his naked body, now spread beneath her. She said uncertainly, "What do I do?"

"As you want, *agape mou*," he said huskily.

Her face was uncertain. Then as she looked down at him, her expression changed. Lowering her head, she whispered, "Don't move a muscle."

She kissed him, entwining his tongue with hers. A shiver went through him and he started to lift his arms around him. Punishingly, she ripped her lips away. "No." Grabbing his wrists, she pushed his arms down firmly into the mattress. "Don't move. And don't say a word!"

He started to reply, then saw her glare.

When she saw his surrender, she gave a satisfied nod and then kissed him again, lowering her lips to his. She was careful to let no other part of their bodies touch, teasing him.

It was hard not to move or speak, when all he wanted to do was wrap his arms around her. She kissed his rough, bristly chin, then down his neck, flicking her tongue over his Adam's apple, caressing down his collarbone to his muscular chest. He felt the delicious warmth of her breath on each nipple. He held his breath as she lowered her head, swirling her tongue around him, drawing him further into her warm, sensual mouth as she suckled him.

And all the while, she was careful not to touch any other part of his body. His shaft was hard, bucking and swaying toward her desperately. Glancing down at him, she smiled: a very smug feminine smile. As if she not only accepted her total power over him in this moment, but she also relished it.

"Holly," he breathed, reaching for her.

"No," she said sharply, pressing down his wrists against the pillow. "If you move again..."

"If I do?"

A strange look came over her face, and she looked him straight in the eye. "You won't feel what you're about to feel."

With an intake of breath, he blinked, then gave her a slow nod, keeping his wrists against the pillow, where she'd pressed them. Her intent gaze burned through him as she slowly lowered her head, sucking on his earlobes, then down the edge of his throat, nibbling on the sensitive corner between his neck and shoulder. She watched how his body reacted, and he saw her triumph.

As she kissed her way down his body, he vowed that soon, very soon—

Then all rational thought disappeared as, never taking her eyes from his, she slowly lowered her head between his legs.

He couldn't look away from the sight of her beautiful, angelic face as her full, swollen, ruby-red lips lowered to take in his hard, throbbing shaft. Her pink tongue snaked out to lick the drop of opalescent liquid at the tip. Then she licked her lips, and murmured, "Mmm…"

He sucked in his breath, staring at her in shock. What had happened to the shy virgin of last Christmas Eve? This woman seemed sure of herself, and ready and able to torture him with his own desire for her.

He held his breath as he watched her take the tip of him into her wet, soft mouth, swirling him with her tongue. Then she took him in deeper, and deeper still. He felt her small hand run exploratively beneath the shaft, juggling him as she sucked him more deeply into the sweet heaven of her mouth. She peeked up at him, and he felt, rather than saw, her satisfied smile.

He could take no more. With a strangled groan, he reached for her, ignoring her weak protest, "I told you not to move!"

He picked her up by the hips as if she weighed nothing, lifted her over his shaft, then slowly lowered her, impaling her inch by delicious inch. With a gasp, she swayed against him, and the sensuality of even that simple movement pounded through his veins. He released her hips, to give her freedom of movement, praying she wouldn't move, praying that she would.

She answered both his prayers when she leaned forward, gripping his shoulders. She closed her eyes, holding still. But just as he started to exhale, she began to move, sliding over him, riding him slowly at first, but then with increasing rhythm. Watching her generous breasts sway over him as she moved, with their tight, deep pink nipples, was too much for him. He closed his eyes, tilting back his head, fighting to keep control. But the image remained. He was lost in the incredible sensation, in pleasure such as he'd never felt before, pleasure he'd never imagined.

She rode him harder and faster, pounding him, until he filled not just her hot wet core, but the universe itself, which began to spin all around him. Finally, gripping his shoulders, she gasped his name.

That pushed him off the edge, and catapulted him into the sky. He thrust one last time, then exploded inside her. He heard a low voice, rising to a ragged shout, crying out her name…and realized to his shock that it was his own.

She collapsed over him, their naked, sweaty, slick bodies intertwined and tangled on the bed. He held her, kissing her temple, and cradled her close. He was lost, he thought. He was found.

His eyes flew open in the darkness. As he held his wife, who'd fallen asleep cradled in his arms, all he could think was that he'd tasted the sweetest drug of his life. But if he consumed too much of it, it would destroy him. There was another name for something like that.

Poison.

CHAPTER TEN

MARRIAGE TO STAVROS was wonderful. Incredible. Better than Holly had ever dreamed.

At first.

After their wedding, they spent a few honeymoon days touring the city with their baby. They'd visited the big Christmas tree at Rockefeller Center, drunk hot cocoa, seen all the festive lights. Stavros had insisted on taking them shopping. When she'd told him they wouldn't need any winter clothes, since her former employer in London had promised to arrange for her possessions to be boxed and sent from Switzerland, Stavros had shrugged. "It's my duty to provide for my wife and child. Not just my duty—my pleasure."

He'd looked so serious and determined, it would have been churlish to refuse.

But instead of just buying her and the baby a few things, as Holly had expected, Stavros had gone as crazy as a contestant in a game show trying to throw as many items in his shopping cart as possible before the timer sounded. Only in this case, he wasn't shopping in a discount mart, but the most expensive boutiques and department stores in the city, and there were endless supplies of carts with no buzzer to stop them.

Finally, after they had more clothes than they'd need in a lifetime of New York winters, he'd taken them back to the chauffeured Rolls-Royce. Even then, instead of returning to the penthouse, her husband had told the driver to take them to the biggest toy store in Manhattan, where, like some darkly sexy Santa, he bought cartloads of toys for Freddie—baseball gear, books, games, an expensive train set, a teddy bear bigger than Stavros himself.

"Freddie's just a baby," Holly had protested, laughing. "He can't play with any of that stuff!"

"Not yet. But soon," he'd replied, kissing her. As his driver arranged for the toys to be delivered to the penthouse, Stavros looked at Holly, his black eyes suddenly hungry. Leaning forward, he stroked through Holly's long red hair beneath her pink knit cap and whispered in her ear, "Let's also get some things we can play with now."

Their exhausted baby had fallen asleep in his car seat by the time they'd arrived at a ridiculously expensive lingerie boutique. Holly had stared at the mannequins in the windows in shocked fascination, before ducking her head, blushing at the image of all the demi bras, garter belts, and crotchless panties that she might have called cheap, except they obviously were not. Aside from her wedding lingerie, which had been procured by the wedding planner, Holly had always purchased simple, sensible cotton bras and panties from places like Wal-Mart or Target.

Reluctantly walking into the French lingerie boutique with Stavros pushing a baby stroller, she'd felt nervous and out of place. When she'd looked at a price tag, she'd gasped and turned around, intending to walk straight back out again.

"Where are you going?" her husband had said, grinning as he grabbed the stroller handle.

She'd looked at him incredulously. "It's two hundred dollars!"

"So?"

"For a *pair of panties*!"

"I would pay far more than that," Stavros had said huskily, running his hand along the sleeve of her long, sleek black coat he'd just bought her at Dior, "to see you in them."

Her blush had felt like a raging fire, and she'd glanced right and left, hoping the salesgirls, all as glamorous as French supermodels, hadn't heard. Then her husband leaned forward and whispered what he planned to do to her later that night, and she was relieved that Freddie was still sleeping in the stroller so his innocent ears wouldn't hear.

"And," Stavros had said when he finally pulled away, "jewelry."

"What could I possibly need more than this?" she'd blurted out, lifting her left hand, with its huge, bulky, platinum-set diamond on her ring finger.

Her husband had given a low laugh. "Oh, my sweet wife," he'd said, cupping her cheek. He ran his thumb lightly along her lower lip, which was still swollen from their lovemaking the previous night. That simple touch made her tingle from her mouth to her breasts and lower still. "You will have rubies as red as your lips. Emeralds bright as your eyes." He'd looked at her with sensual, heavy-lidded eyes. "I will see you naked in my bed, wearing only diamonds that sparkle like Christmas morning…"

And he had.

Holly shivered now, remembering.

For the last three weeks, since their marriage, he'd made love to her every night. Somehow, each night was more spectacular than the last. She didn't understand how it was possible.

Perhaps it helped that she was no longer so exhausted from waking up multiple times with their baby throughout the night. As if even Freddie felt the new stability and security of their lives, he'd started sleeping better and longer at night than he had before. And she also had Eleni's help now.

So, almost against her will, Holly had found herself spending the holiday season as a princess in a New York penthouse, draped in jewels and expensive designer clothes, a lady of leisure whose only job was to cuddle her baby by day and be seduced by her husband at night. A life so wonderful it made her feel guilty, wondering what she'd done to deserve so much, when other people she knew had so much less.

So she'd asked Stavros if, instead of giving each other gifts for Christmas this year, they could donate money to charitable causes. He'd grudgingly agreed, seeing how important it was to her.

Holly was happy to make homemade Christmas gifts—knitted booties for Freddie, and a red felt star for Stavros, in the Marlowe family tradition. Whenever her former employer got around to sending her old Christmas decorations from Switzerland, Holly couldn't wait to add her husband's star to her family's heirloom garland.

Wrapping his red felt star in homemade wrapping paper, Holly had hidden it amid the branches of the brightly lit white Christmas tree in their bedroom, and waited for the right moment to surprise him.

But after the first delicious week of their honeymoon, things seemed to change between them. Stavros went back to work. Instead of spending all day with him, she saw him only in the middle of the night, when he would wake her up to make passionate love to her. By dawn, when Holly woke, Stavros was gone again.

Finally, out of desperation, Holly had put the baby in his stroller and gone to the offices of Minos International, hoping to see him, maybe take him to lunch. But Stavros had been deep in a conference meeting and barely spoke two words to her, seeming only annoyed by the interruption. Rejected, she'd gone to talk to her old coworkers. She'd relished the other secretaries' excited congratulations and demands to see Holly's spectacular diamond ring. They'd invited her to lunch, and she'd accepted happily.

But seated at their usual delicatessen, the conversation had dwindled. The other secretaries, who'd once been her colleagues, didn't really know how to act now she was the CEO's wife. A few were clearly trying to repress burning jealousy, while others seemed merely uncertain what to say.

Holly yearned to show them that she hadn't changed since her marriage, and was still the same person. But how?

As she ate her favorite Reuben sandwich with dill pickle, she listened to the other women talk about their problems. One had an ex not paying child support, another was falling behind on medical bills, another couldn't find good day care. Then their eyes inevitably fell on Holly's huge diamond ring, and baby Freddie, sleeping in his expensive, top-of-the-line stroller. Holly could see what they were thinking: lucky Holly and her baby were set for life.

Cheeks burning, Holly had said quickly, "If there's anything I can do to help—"

"No, no," her former friends had said, waving her off. "We'll be fine."

"Perhaps my husband could give you a raise…" But before Holly even finished her sentence, she knew she'd made a mistake. Her friends had stared at her, quietly offended.

"We're fine, Holly."

"We don't need your charity," another had muttered, sucking down the last of her soda noisily through a straw as she glared at the floor.

The lunch had gone downhill after that. When it was finally over, Holly had suggested they make plans soon. But none of her old friends seemed particularly keen to set a date.

"Don't worry," Audrey, her closest office friend, had whispered as they left. "They'll get used to it. Just give them a little time."

Holly hoped she was right. She still felt a lump in her throat, remembering that awkward lunch.

But at least she and her sister were friends again. Though Nicole hadn't told her much, apparently Oliver's financial situation had improved. Either they'd learned to live on less, or Oliver must have found a job. Either way, she was happy to have her sister back. Nicole now answered all her texts, and had even visited Holly last week at the penthouse.

But when Holly asked how things were going,

Nicole had given a wan smile. "You know how marriage is. Or at least," she'd sighed, "you will."

And maybe Nicole had had a point.

Because Holly felt like something had already changed in her marriage. She and Stavros had started in such bliss, with such joyful days together. It hadn't been just shopping. She'd gotten lots of his time and attention. She'd watched him play with their baby. They'd spent hours talking, hours just kissing—in front of the fire, on the sidewalk as they pushed the stroller…he kissed her anywhere—but somewhere along the line, something shocking had happened.

She'd fallen in love with him.

It was the purest bad luck, a horrible coincidence, that the very day she realized she loved him, and started trying to find the words to tell him, Stavros had become utterly distracted at work by the acquisition of some billion-dollar tech company.

He wasn't avoiding her deliberately, she told herself. Of course not. Why would he? True, he'd told her he had some issues about fearing love and commitment, but that was all in the past. He'd married her, hadn't he? He'd promised to be faithful forever. That proved he was more than ready to open up his heart!

But Stavros had run his company for nearly twenty years. That mattered to him, too. He'd tried to explain the new technology to her, and why Minos International needed to acquire it, but Holly's eyes had crossed with boredom halfway through the first sentence.

Or maybe she just hadn't wanted to understand it. What she wanted was for him to finish the deal, so he could stop spending eighteen-hour days at the office and spend time with her and Freddie again.

Like tonight. For the umpteenth time, Holly glanced at the clock over the mantel in the great room of the penthouse. It was nearly ten now, and Stavros had been at the office since dawn. He hadn't seen his son before he left; and now, Freddie had been asleep for hours.

"Is that all, Mrs. Holly?"

Looking up from the chair where she was reading a magazine, Holly saw Eleni. The white-haired Greek woman, who'd by now become part of their family, still insisted on calling her by that formal name. "Yes, Eleni. Thank you."

She nodded. "*Kalinixta*, Mrs. Holly."

"Good night. Thank you." After the older woman headed to her suite downstairs, Holly tried to read, watching the clock, waiting always to hear Stavros at the door.

Finally, she yawned and stretched. Letting the magazine drop against her chest, she looked out at the nighttime city through the wide windows.

She just had to be patient, she told herself. After his business deal was done, their marriage would return to the way it had been during their honeymoon. He would have time for their family again.

And Holly would finally tell him she loved him.

She closed her eyes, hope rising in her heart as she pictured the scene. And then—and then... he'd tell her he loved her, too.

She hoped.

What if he didn't?

Nervousness roiled through her. She set down the magazine on the end table, then rose to her feet and paced in front of the windows. She stopped. There was nothing to be gained by being afraid, she told herself. She'd just have to be brave, and trust everything would be all right. Her husband would love her back. Of course he would.

Holly pushed away her fear. Glancing at the clock over the mantel, she saw that it was just past midnight. It was December twenty-third. Just a few minutes into her twenty-eighth birthday. She brightened.

At least she'd finally get time with him at the surprise party he'd promised her. Could it be called a surprise party when she was counting on it, longing for it? She smiled. He hadn't said a word about what he'd planned, but Holly knew it would be wonderful.

Turning off the lamp, she looked around the quiet, lonely penthouse. It was dark, except for the lights of the Christmas tree shining in the great room.

She wished she didn't have to go to bed alone. But she comforted herself with thoughts of tomorrow. As she brushed her teeth in the enormous, gleaming master bathroom, she closed her eyes in anticipation, imagining her friends and family celebrating together. They'd talk and laugh and eat birthday cake, and all awkwardness with her former colleagues would be smoothed over. Nicole and Oliver would be there. And best of all, she'd finally have time with her husband.

Looking at herself in the mirror, she came to a sudden decision.

Tomorrow at the party, she'd tell Stavros she loved him.

Yes. Tomorrow. Smiling, she peeked into the nursery to check on her sleeping baby, then padded softly back to climb into bed. Glancing at the empty bed on Stavros's side, she looked out the window and made a birthday wish that he'd finish the deal tonight, and starting tomorrow, he'd never be gone so much again. And why shouldn't it happen? Her smile became dreamy. When she woke up, they'd celebrate her birthday, and the day after that would be Christmas Eve. And sometime in the middle of the night tonight, Stavros would wake her with a kiss, and make passionate love to her.

She fell asleep when her head hit the pillow, and spent the night dreaming of her husband's hot kisses.

When she woke up the morning of her birthday, she saw the sky was blue outside, and the sun was bright and gold. She looked over at Stavros's side of the bed, and saw it hadn't been slept in. Stavros had never come home last night at all.

Holly heard echoes of Oliver's laughing voice. *Minos men are selfish to the bone. We do what we like, and everyone else be damned.*

And worse, Stavros's words. *Love always has*

a winner and a loser. A conqueror and a conquered.

If she loved him, and he didn't love her back, which would she be?

With a chill, Holly knew the heartbreaking answer.

When his eyes opened, Stavros sat up straight from the sofa.

Seeing the full morning sunlight coming from the window, he gave a low curse, then stood up so fast he almost felt dizzy. His muscles were cramped from a long night spent hunched over the conference-room table, and a few hours of unsettling sleep on his office sofa had left his spine and joints out of place.

He stretched painfully, blinking with exhaustion as he looked around his spacious private office. Piles of papers covered his large, usually pristine black desk, along with empty takeout cartons, the remnants of the kung pao shrimp and broccoli beef his support staff had arranged to be delivered for the negotiating team's dinner at midnight. Stavros had brought the cartons in here to eat privately as he read through the other company's last-minute counteroffer, striking out lines with his red pen before he returned to the conference room to compare notes with his lawyers.

Sometime around 4:00 a.m., he'd realized his brain was in a fog. So he'd stretched out on his sofa. He'd only meant to rest his eyes for a moment, but now it was—looking at his smartwatch, Stavros cursed aloud—nearly eight o'clock. He was supposed to meet back with his team in ten minutes.

Stavros should have texted Holly to let her know he wouldn't be coming home. He should have—

He should do nothing. The cold voice spoke calmly in his soul. Keep his distance. Let her know that their marriage could never be more than a domestic and sexual partnership. Romantic love would never—could never—be a part of it. He wanted Holly to realize this without him having to tell her. The last thing he wanted to do was hurt her.

The first week of their marriage had been the best week of his life. Pleasure, enjoyment, friendship...and mind-blowing sex. He'd been happy with her. He'd forgotten to be so guarded. He'd spent hours with her, not just in bed, but talking about his past. About his feelings. About everything.

And he'd caught Holly looking at him with wistful longing in her beautiful emerald eyes. Something more than admiration. Something far more than his dark soul deserved.

It had shaken him to the core. He'd crossed a line he shouldn't have crossed. He couldn't let Holly fall in love with him. He couldn't. And not just because he'd never love her back.

Love was tragedy. There were only two ways love could end—betrayal, or death.

It was a thought made all the sharper today, Stavros thought now. The one-year anniversary of when he'd gotten his fatal diagnosis last year. He'd lived, against all odds. But the miracle could so easily have not happened. And though his last medical scan had showed him in complete remission, one never knew. He could die of something else. Or Holly could.

How could anyone think of loving each other, knowing it could only end in tragedy?

So he'd forced himself to turn away from all the joy and light his wife had brought to his days. He'd grimly reassembled the walls that guarded his soul. He couldn't let her love him. He had to hold the line. He couldn't be so cruel as to lure her into loving him when he knew it would only bring her pain. He had to fight it.

He couldn't bear the thought of ever seeing Holly suffer. He had to protect her—even from himself.

But how could he pull away, without making her feel the sting of rejection?

He'd grabbed onto the negotiations for this business deal with force. It was an amazing excuse to create some distance from his wife.

Although spending an entire night apart was a little *too* much distance. Going into the private bathroom of his office, he brushed his teeth, then spat out the toothpaste. He looked bleakly in the mirror.

There were dark circles under his eyes from stress and lack of sleep. He missed Holly. He missed his son. He wanted to be home.

He had to remind himself, again and again, that he was staying away for their sakes. Because if Holly fell in love with him, sooner or later she'd demand he love her back. When he couldn't, she'd ask for a divorce. And just like that, their family would be destroyed.

Or maybe she wouldn't ask for a divorce. Maybe it would be even worse. Maybe she'd stay in their marriage, trapped forever in silent desperation.

Last year, when Stavros had thought he was

dying, he'd feared leaving Holly behind as a brokenhearted widow. How much worse would it be if instead, she loved him without hope for the rest of her life, making their marriage a sort of living death?

Stavros's shoulders ached as he took a quick, hot shower, trying to wash his churning feelings away. Getting out, he toweled off and pulled on the spare suit that he kept cleaned and pressed in his closet.

Quickly shaving, he avoided his own eyes in the mirror. He hurried out of his private bathroom, already late, trying to focus his mind only on the upcoming conference call—

Stavros stopped flat when he saw his wife waiting in the middle of his private office.

"Hello," Holly said, gripping the handle of the baby stroller.

"Hello," he replied, shocked. The one time she'd visited the Minos building since their marriage, he'd made sure he was too busy to talk to her.

Now, against his will, his eyes drank her in hungrily. Gone were the beige, baggy suits she'd worn as a secretary, and the casual jeans and sweater she'd worn in the Swiss chalet. Now she dressed like the wife of a billionaire CEO.

She wore a sleek black cashmere jacket over a white button-down shirt, fitted black pants and knee-high black leather boots. Diamond studs sparkled in her ears. "What are you doing here, Holly?"

She ducked her head. "I was in the area. Nicole asked me out for coffee." She gave a shy smile. "For obvious reasons."

Obvious? How obvious? Then he remembered. "To thank you? So Oliver got the paperwork."

"Paperwork?"

"For the ten million."

Holly's expression was blank. "What are you talking about?"

Stavros frowned. If his financial gift to his cousin wasn't the obvious reason, what was? "The annuity I arranged."

Her lips parted. "You're giving Oliver money?"

"Don't worry," he assured her. "The contract is airtight. He just gets a million up front, and each year they remain married, he'll get another. But only if Nicole signs a statement each year that he's keeping her happy."

Instead of looking reassured, she looked shocked. "You're *paying* Oliver to stay married to my sister?"

"Just for the first ten years," he said, confused.

Why did Holly seem so upset? "I know you can't be happy unless the people you love are happy, too. The money is a pittance. So I took care of it."

Her face was incredulous. "And you think paying that—that *gigolo* to stay married to my sister will make her happy?"

"Doesn't it?"

"Love is what makes a marriage! Not money!"

Stavros didn't like where this conversation was going. His fear about making Holly love him, about breaking her heart and ruining her life, started pressing against him as heavily as an anvil. Folding his arms, he said tightly, "Fine. I'll tell my lawyer to cancel the annuity. Is that all?"

"No, it's not all!" Her lovely heart-shaped face was pale as she lifted her chin. "Why didn't you come home last night?"

Her lips were pink and chapped, as if she'd chewed them for hours. Her green eyes were vulnerable, troubled with shadows. Had he put those shadows there?

The thought of hurting her made him sick inside. It made him angry. He glared at her. "I've been closing an important deal. As you know. Which is what I need to be doing now. So if you'll excuse me..."

But she blocked him with the stroller, where their baby was babbling and waving his pudgy arms. "And that's all you have to say to me? After you were gone all night? Without a single message?"

A low Greek curse rose to his throat. It was all he could do to choke it back. "Holly, I'm working. I'm sorry I didn't call. Now please let me go."

She took a deep breath. "Stavros, we need to talk."

But the last thing he wanted to do right now was talk to her. She was blocking him from where he needed to be. And if he stayed, he'd only be forced to say things that might hurt her.

Why couldn't she take the hint that he didn't want or deserve her love? Did he have to spell it out for her?

Stavros nodded scornfully toward the sofa where he'd slept a few uncomfortable hours. "What is it? Do you think I was here all night with some other woman, making hot, sweet love to her? You think I'm like all the other Minos men—after just a few weeks, I'm already bored of my wife?"

Her beautiful face went white, then red. She whispered, "You don't have to be cruel."

Grinding his teeth, Stavros clawed back his dark hair. "Look, if you don't trust me, why are we even married?"

Folding her arms, she glared at him in turn. "Yes, why, when Freddie and I barely see you anymore?"

Exhaling with a flare of nostrils, Stavros glanced at his watch, imagining the conference call had already started. If he didn't hurry, it might cost his company millions of dollars. But that wasn't the reason he had to get away from her, from the bewildered suffering he saw in her expressive green eyes.

"Fine," he growled. "We'll talk. Tonight."

"All right." Biting her lip, she lowered her arms and said uncertainly, "I just remembered. Today is the anniversary of your diagnosis last year. How are you feeling?"

"Never better," he said shortly. "I got a clean bill of health last month. Still in complete remission."

A warm smile lit up her face. "I'm so glad. I wish you'd told me you—"

"Look, Holly, I don't mean to be rude, but can this wait? I have a conference room full of lawyers waiting."

"Yes. Yes, of course." She blushed a little,

looking sweetly shy. "I'm looking forward to tonight. Will you be home early?"

"Unlikely," he said shortly, wondering why she'd be excited for him to come home tonight so they could argue, and he could tell her, to her face, what she should have already known—that he'd never love her. "I've got to go."

"All right." She came closer, her eyes glowing, her expression caught between hope and fear. "There's something I want to tell you. Something important. I—"

But as she looked at him, something made her expression change. Something made her back away.

"Never mind," she choked out, shaking her head. "It doesn't matter. I'll see you later—"

And she turned, and fled his office with the baby.

Stavros exhaled, relieved. Maybe he'd been wrong. Holly wasn't falling for him. She was too smart to give her love to a man who didn't deserve it. And what could a man like Stavros ever do to truly deserve her love and light?

He couldn't. So there was no point in trying. It would only lead to loss and darkness—

Pushing away the twist in his gut—it felt like being punched—he clenched his hands into fists.

Striding out of his office, he barked at one of his assistants, "Call my lawyer. I want the deal with my cousin canceled at once."

He didn't slow down to hear the reply. Because if there was anything his illness had taught him, it was that life was short. You had to do the important things now, because you never knew if there would be a tomorrow. You had to know what was really, truly important.

And blocking out all emotion from his soul, Stavros hurried to the conference room, where a billion-dollar deal waited.

CHAPTER ELEVEN

SHE'D ALMOST MADE a horrible mistake.

Holly was still shaking as she pushed the stroller down the long city block toward the small café where she was supposed to meet her sister for coffee.

She'd been heartbroken when she'd woken up to discover Stavros had never come home last night. When her sister had invited her out for her birthday, she'd chosen a café near his office. She'd gone there with her heart on fire, half longing for him, half hurt.

And she'd nearly blurted out that she loved him. Surely, once he knew that, once he understood that he held her heart in his hands, he would treat her with greater care?

But looking at his coldly handsome face in his office, Holly had suddenly realized that he wouldn't. Because he already knew.

He knew she loved him. But he didn't want her to speak the words aloud.

Because then he'd be forced to admit he didn't love her back.

Now, hurt and grief threatened to overwhelm her as she maneuvered the stroller down the Midtown sidewalk, crowded with last-minute holiday shoppers. The windows were full of brightly decorated Christmas scenes. But in her current mood, as her eyes fell on the vestiges of melted snow in the shadowed places on the sidewalk, the city seemed gray and dirty. Just like her dreams.

Her baby gave a little plaintive cry from the stroller, snapping Holly back to reality. Stopping on the corner to wait for the crosswalk light, she caressed Freddie, even as she fiercely blinked back tears. Reaching into his blankets, she found his pacifier and popped it back into his mouth, causing him to settle back into the stroller.

Straightening, Holly took a deep breath. As the light changed, she crossed the street surrounded by happy, smiling crowds laden with holiday gifts. Looking down at Freddie in the stroller, she felt her heart in her throat as Stavros's words came back to her.

Love always has a winner, and a loser. A conqueror and a conquered. I decided long ago I never wanted to be either.

She'd thought, when Stavros married her, he'd changed his mind. But he hadn't. He just wanted them to be a family.

So did she.

Holly took a deep breath. Maybe she could love him enough for both of them, she tried to tell herself. If Stavros treated her well, if he cherished her, couldn't that be enough? As long as he was a good father, and a good husband? As long as he spent time with them? Which she was sure he would, as soon as this business deal was over.

Stavros might not be in love with her, but he cared about her. After all, he'd arranged a big birthday party for her tonight. A sort of surprise party, their first social event as a married couple. All their friends and family would be there.

She just had to focus on the positive. She was twenty-eight now, a married lady with a baby. It was time to grow up.

She could live without her husband's love.

Lifting her mouth into a smile as she reached the café, she pushed the stroller inside. She saw her little sister sitting at a nearby table, her face in her hands. Next to her on the table, there was a small birthday gift beside a large coffee mug.

Holly parked the stroller beside the small table. "Nicole?"

Her sister looked up. Tears were streaking her face.

"What is it?" Holly cried, horrified.

"I just got a call from Oliver," she whispered. "Stavros canceled the annuity. So he's leaving me."

"Oh, no!"

"He's moving in with someone else." Her voice choked. "A rich older woman who can give him the lifestyle he deserves."

Sitting in a nearby chair, Holly pulled Nicole into her arms as her baby sister cried against her shoulder.

"I'm so sorry, Nicole," she whispered, rubbing her back. "This is my fault. I told Stavros he shouldn't pay Oliver to be married to you. You deserve more. Marriage should be about love, not money." But as her sister's crying only increased, Holly blurted out, "I'm sorry."

Nicole pulled away, wiping her eyes. "This *is* your fault, Holly. Your fault for trying to take care of me, even when I didn't deserve it. You fault for always thinking I was wonderful, even when I was a total jerk. Even when I stole the man you wanted."

"Stole…" Nicole had tried to steal Stavros? Holly stared at her, confused. Then she understood and exhaled in relief. "Oh, you mean Oliver."

"I knew you had a huge crush on him as his secretary," Nicole sniffed. "But I still took him. And now the universe is punishing me as I deserve."

"You're wrong," Holly said. "Oliver was never mine. The romantic dream kept me company, that was all. It was never real. You didn't take anything from me, Nicole. You don't deserve anything but love!"

"That's what I mean," her little sister said, shaking her head as she gave a tremulous smile. "Even when I've been horrible to you, you find a way to see me in the best possible light." She wiped her tears. "When Mom and Dad died, you gave up everything to raise me. I never appreciated that. It's only now I realize how selfish I've been."

"Oh, Nicole…"

Her sister took a deep breath, leaning back into her own chair. "It's time for me to strike out on my own. The fact that Oliver has left makes it easier."

"You don't have to be alone. Come stay with us for Christmas. There's plenty of room!"

Nicole shook her head. "I'm going to visit my old roommate up in Vermont. Her family has a ski resort, you know, a little one, which they operate on a shoestring. I need some time away, to figure out what to do with my life." She paused. "Besides. You have your own problems."

"What are you talking about?"

"Like I said. You always see the best in people, Holly. Even when they don't deserve it. You see what you want to see with those rose-colored glasses. Oliver. Me." She tilted her head. "Stavros."

"You think I don't see him how he really is?" she said slowly.

Her sister's eyes challenged her. "Do you love him?"

Holly took a deep breath. The truth forced itself from her lips. "Yes."

"Does he love you?"

In spite of Holly's efforts to convince herself she didn't need her husband's love, a lump rose to her throat. She looked away.

"That's what I thought," Nicole said quietly. Putting her hand on her shoulder, she repeated the same words Holly had just said to her. "You deserve more."

Suddenly, Holly was the one who was crying. Angry at herself, she wiped her eyes. "We can still be happy. Stavros just loves me differently, that's all. He cares for me. He shows it through his actions. Like the party tonight..."

Nicole frowned. "What party?"

She smiled through her tears. "You don't need to pretend. I know he's throwing me a birthday party. He insisted on doing it, since I didn't want a wedding reception. There's no way he wouldn't invite you." Holly's lower lip trembled. She desperately needed to feel some hope. "So you can tell me about it. It's not a surprise."

"I'm not trying to keep anything a surprise. There's no party, Holly."

She stared at her sister. As a waiter came and asked if they needed anything, Nicole shook her head. Holly didn't even look at him.

"No party?" she said numbly.

"I'm sorry. Maybe he's doing something else to surprise you?" Her sister tried to smile as she pushed the small, brightly wrapped present toward her. "Here. Wrapped in birthday paper, like you always wanted." She smiled ruefully.

"Not Christmas paper, which you've always had to put up with from me."

Holly looked down at the present. It was beautifully wrapped, in pink and emerald, her two favorite colors.

"What's inside is even better. Something I know you've always wanted but were never selfish enough to admit it. Open it."

Slowly, Holly obeyed. And gasped.

Inside the box, nestled in white tissue paper, was the precious gold-star necklace that had once belonged to their mother.

"Told you I'd find it," Nicole said smugly. "It was tucked in my old high-school sweatshirt buried at the bottom of my keepsake box."

A lump rose in Holly's throat as she lifted the necklace. Their mother had worn it every day. It had been a gift from their father, who'd always called Louisa his north star.

"I know you wanted me to have it, so I'd never lose my way," her sister said in a low voice. "But I think you need it more than I do now."

Nicole's husband had left her, they'd soon be going through a divorce, but she still thought Holly needed it more? Her hand tightened around the necklace as she said hoarsely, "Why?"

"You told me love makes a marriage, not

money." Nicole shook her head. "Are you really going to spend your life waiting for Stavros to love you—waiting hopelessly, until you die?"

Holly stared at her little sister in the small New York café. As customers and waiters bustled around them, the smell of coffee and peppermint mochas in the air, the heat of the café made her feel sweaty and hot, then clammy and cold.

Then she realized it wasn't the café, but her heart.

She'd spent her whole life taking care of others, imagining herself in love with unobtainable men—first Oliver, then Stavros. Even now, she'd been ready to settle for a dream to keep her warm, so she didn't feel so hopeless and alone, rather than be brave enough to hold out for the real thing.

Her gaze fell on Freddie, wrapped in blankets, sucking his pacifier in the stroller. Was this the example she wanted to set for her son? That marriage meant one person martyred by love, and the other a tyrant over it?

Love always has a winner and a loser. A conqueror and a conquered.

Which one was she?

Closing her eyes, Holly took a deep breath.

Then she slowly opened them.

No. She wouldn't settle. Not anymore. Not when her and Freddie's whole lives were at stake.

And Stavros's, too.

He'd never wanted to hurt her. He'd said from the beginning that he had no desire to be a conqueror. And yet her love for him would make him one.

Holly reached up to clasp her mother's necklace around her neck. She touched the gold star gently at her collarbone. No. She wanted love, real love. She wanted what her parents had had.

Love made a marriage. Not money. Not sex. Not even friendship. Only love.

And she wouldn't, couldn't, spend the rest of her life without it.

It was nearly midnight when Stavros arrived home.

For a moment, he leaned his head against the door, exhausted. He'd only slept three hours in the last forty-eight. But the deal was struck at last. He was done.

At least until the next deal. He was already considering a potential acquisition of a company in Pittsburgh that had developed an AI-based sales networking platform. He would call his lawyers about it tomorrow. With any luck, they could strike first, while his competitors were still lazing over Christmas presents and turkey dinners.

Entering the dark, silent penthouse, he turned on a light in the foyer. He nearly jumped when he saw his wife sitting on the sofa of the great room, staring into the pale flames of the gas fireplace. Beside her, the lights of the Christmas tree sparkled wanly.

"What are you doing up so late?" he said uneasily. It couldn't be anything good.

Slowly, she rose to face him. She wasn't in pajamas, as one might expect, but was fully dressed, and not in the sleek designer clothes he'd bought her, but the simple sweater and jeans she'd worn when they'd left Switzerland last month.

"We need to talk."

"So you said. But it's been a long day. Can we do it tomorrow?" *Or never.* He raked a hand through his dark hair, setting down his laptop bag as he gave her a small smile. "The deal is signed."

"Oh?" She came toward him. "So you're done?"

"Yes."

She paused. "So you'll be home more—"

"There's always another deal, Holly." He hung up his black Italian cashmere coat. "There's a new potential acquisition brewing. I'll need to leave for the office early tomorrow."

Her lips parted. "But tomorrow's Christmas Eve. And you just got home. We haven't seen you for weeks—"

"I'm CEO of a major corporation, Holly." His voice was more harsh than he intended, but he was tired. He didn't want to hear her complaints. He didn't want to feel guilty right now—or feel anything at all. "This is how we pay for this lifestyle. For all your jewels and fine clothes."

Holly lifted her chin. "I never asked for any of that."

She was right, which left him no room to negotiate or blame her. It irritated him. "Look, I'm exhausted. Our talk is just going to have to wait."

"Until when?"

He shrugged. "Until I have time." Which, with luck, he never would. All he needed to do was line up endless mergers and acquisitions, endless reams of work, and he'd have an excellent excuse never to have to tell her out loud that he didn't love her, or see her beautiful face break into a million pieces.

But as he turned away, he was stopped by her voice.

"Do you know what today is?"

Scowling, he glanced back. She'd better not bring up last year's fatal diagnosis again. "The day I signed a new billion-dollar deal?"

She gave him a thin smile. "My birthday."

He blinked, then a savage curse went through his mind. Of course. December twenty-third. Her birthday.

Now he felt guiltier than ever, which only made him angrier. He'd totally forgotten her birthday, and his promise to throw her a party. He was the one who'd first insisted on throwing her one, like a big shot. Now he looked like a flake. Now he'd let her down.

Stavros hated the disappointment in her green eyes—the hollow accusation there. It was the same way his mother had looked at his father when Aristides failed her, time and time again. As a boy, Stavros had always wondered why his mother put up with such treatment.

Now, he was somehow in his father's place. He hadn't cheated, but he'd accidentally lied.

There was no party. He wouldn't, couldn't, bear to think of himself as the villain in this equation.

"I'm sorry," he said tightly. Admitting a mistake was difficult for him. He resisted the temptation to make excuses, to blame her for expecting too much when he'd been swamped with the business deal. Setting his jaw, he said only, "I forgot about the party. I will have my secretary arrange it as soon as possible."

"Your secretary?"

His jaw tightened further. "Would you rather have a gift? Jewels? A trip?"

She took a deep breath. He saw tears in her eyes. "What I wanted was your time."

Seeing her tears hurt him so badly, he couldn't help lashing out. "Then you had unrealistic expectations. Did you really think our honeymoon could last forever?"

"Yes," she whispered. She looked down at the big diamond ring sparkling on her left hand. It glittered like the tears in her eyes. "I love you, Stavros. Can you ever love me?"

It had finally come. The moment he'd dreaded. He wanted to avoid the question.

But looking at her miserable face, he had to tell her the truth.

"No," he said quietly. "I'm sorry, Holly. It's

nothing personal. I told you. I'm just not made that way."

Her shoulders sagged. Then she looked up with a tremulous smile. "I'm sorry, too. This is what you meant, isn't it? About the conqueror and the conquered."

"Yes." His heart felt radioactive. Grimly, he buried it in lead, beneath ten feet of ice. "I never wanted you to love me."

"I know. And I was so mad when you told me this would happen." Her expression was wistful. "That I wouldn't be able to resist falling in love with you."

His shoulders felt painfully tight. "You're a good person, Holly. I don't want you to suffer." He pleaded, "Can't you be happy with the life we have? Can't you just take your love back?"

Holly stared at him for a long moment, then slowly shook her head.

"I can't. I can't pretend not to love you. I can't wish it away. I'm sorry. I know I'm putting you in a position you never wanted to be." Blinking fast, she tried to smile through her tears. "It'll be all right."

Stavros frowned, coming closer. He yearned to wrap his arms around her, to comfort her. But how could he, when he himself was the reason she was crying? "It will?"

Holly nodded. "It's time for me to grow up. To see things as they really are." She looked at him. "Not as I wish they could be."

He felt her words like an ice pick through his frozen heart. And it was then that he saw her old overnight bag, sitting by the front door.

"You're leaving me," he whispered, hardly able to believe it.

Looking away, Holly nodded. Tears were streaking her face. "I knew what you were going to say. But I… I guess I just had to hear it aloud. To know there was absolutely no hope."

Reaching forward, he grabbed her shoulders and searched her gaze. "You don't have to leave. I want you to stay…"

She shook her head. "I saw Nicole today. Oliver's left her for another woman. In the past, I would have been scrambling to try to fix her life, to smooth her path. But she doesn't need that anymore. She's stronger than I thought. And you know what? So am I." Lifting her gaze to his, she said simply, "I've been on my own before. I can do it again."

Stavros dropped his hands. "On your own?"

"I once thought the only way I'd be loved was

if I sacrificed myself for others. It's taken all this—" she looked around the elegant, sparsely decorated penthouse "—for me to realize that's not how love works. You can't earn someone's love by giving them your soul. They either love you, or they don't." She gave him a tremulous smile. "It's all right, Stavros. Truly. You'll be better off this way, too. You have nothing to feel bad about."

"Holly, damn it—"

"It's no one's fault." She tried to smile. "Thank you for telling me the truth."

"And this is my reward?" A lump was in his throat. "To have you leave?"

"No one will be surprised when we break up. You gave your baby your name. That's enough." Wiping her eyes, she gave a wry grin. "I mean, come on, a secretary and a billionaire tycoon? No one would ever think *that* marriage could last."

"And Freddie?" he said hoarsely.

A wave of emotion went over Holly's face. But he saw her control it, saw her accept it and master it.

"We'll share custody," she said quietly. "You'll always be in his life." She allowed herself a rueful smile. "Although let's be honest. Working eighteen-hour days, Christmas included, you weren't exactly going to see him much, anyway, were you? Even if we all lived in the same house."

Stavros's heart twisted at the thought of no longer living in the same house as his baby son. But how could he argue with her?

Everything she'd said was true. Just like with her birthday party, he'd made grand promises he hadn't kept. He'd sworn he'd be an amazing father. Then he'd disappeared to the office.

He yearned to reach for her, to drag her into his arms, to kiss her senseless until she agreed to forget this love idea and stay with him forever.

But he was backed into a corner. Holly was leaving him, and there was nothing he could do about it. He couldn't lure or romance her into staying, knowing he'd be stealing her soul and giving nothing back in return. He couldn't be such a monster, allowing her to remain and look at him each day with heartbreaking hope in her eyes, yearning for love he couldn't give.

Nor could he be the spiteful, selfish man his father had been, trying to hold her against her will, by threatening to take custody of Freddie or withholding the five million dollars guaranteed by their prenuptial agreement, in a malicious attempt to punish her, or keep her down.

No.

"Where will you go?" he asked in a small voice.

"Switzerland."

"Tonight? So late?"

"I wasn't sure when you'd get home tonight." She gave a brief smile. "Or even *if* you'd come home."

His eyes tightened. "I explained why I was late."

"It doesn't matter anymore." Her smile was sad. "Freddie and I are booked on the first plane to Zurich tomorrow. It leaves at five. It seemed easier to stay overnight at a hotel by the airport. Eleni's already there with him."

He wouldn't even get to say goodbye to his son? He felt a lump in his throat, a coldness spreading to his chest. He wanted to argue, to demand more time.

Then he looked at Holly. She'd already decided. Once a woman knew what she wanted, what was to be gained from waiting?

He'd never admired her more than he did in this moment.

All he could try to do was accept her decision

better than his own father had. He forced himself to ask the question. "When can I see him again?"

"Anytime you come to Switzerland."

His voice was hoarse as he said, "Take my jet."

Holly looked surprised at his offer, then gave a crooked half grin. "We don't need anything so fancy. Commercial is fine. Just a seat in economy class with my baby in my lap."

Stavros imagined his wife crammed into an uncomfortable middle seat, with four-hundred-pound men on each side of her, and their baby squirming and crying in her lap for nine hours straight. "If you don't want to take my jet, at least fly first class. You don't need to economize. Your prenuptial agreement guarantees—"

"No." She cut him off harshly. "That's Freddie's money."

"I'll always provide for Freddie. The five million is yours."

"I don't want it." Her green eyes were hard. Then she added lightly, "Anyway, first class is no place for a baby. The executives and supermodels up there would smash their champagne flutes and attack us if Freddie started crying. Which he will. His ears always hurt during take-off. You remember how it was when we flew to Greece. And New York."

Their eyes met, and he felt a stab in his chest.

"My jet will take you." He was proud of his matter-of-fact tone.

"It's not necessary—"

"Stop arguing." His voice was flat, brooking no opposition. "You don't need to sleep in a motel 'til morning. You can leave at once. Freddie will be more comfortable. You know it's true."

She sighed. "Thanks," she said slowly. Pulling the huge diamond ring off her finger, she held it out. "This belongs to you."

Reluctantly, he took it. The ten-carat, platinum-set diamond that had been the symbol of forever was now just a cold rock in his hand. He gripped it in his palm.

"I'll have a lawyer contact you after Christmas." She tried to smile. "We'll be civilized."

He'd never felt this wretched, even when his mother had died. As Holly turned to go, he choked out unwillingly, "How can you do this? If you love me, how can you leave?"

She turned back, her eyes full of tears. "If I'm not strong now, I never will be. And we'll both have lifetimes of regret. I know what your childhood did to you. I won't let our son believe all the wrong things about what a marriage is supposed to be. I won't let him grow up crippled like…"

"Like I am?" Stavros said in a low voice.

Coming forward, she kissed his cheek. He felt her warmth, breathed in the scent of vanilla and orange blossoms.

"Be happy," she whispered.

And, picking up her overnight bag, Holly left.

CHAPTER TWELVE

THE NEXT MORNING Stavros woke up to the blaring sound of an alarm on his phone. Without opening his eyes, he reached out for Holly's warmth.

Her side of the bed was cold. And he remembered. Slowly, he opened his eyes.

She was gone.

With a hollow breath, he looked down at his rumpled clothes. He'd fallen into bed last night in his white shirt and black trousers. He hadn't had the energy to change his clothes. He hadn't wanted to think. It was either fall into bed, or into a bottle of whiskey, and the bed had been closer.

But he'd dreamed all night, strange dreams where he was smiling and happy. Beautiful, vibrant dreams in which he'd held his wife's hand, and they'd been together in a wintry valley, making a snowman with their son. Stavros hadn't been afraid to love her. In his dream, he'd fearlessly given her all his heart.

The cobwebs of those dreams taunted him as he stiffly sat up in the cold light. It was Christmas Eve morning. Everything looked gray. His empty bedroom. The city outside. The sky. Gray. All gray.

Except—

His eyes narrowed when he saw a strange flash of color. Something red. Getting out of bed, he padded softly across the marble floor as he reached for something in the branches of the artificial tree. A small Christmas present, wrapped in red homemade paper with a red bow.

To my husband.

His heart twisted. For a moment, he stared at it, like he'd discovered a poisonous snake amid the branches. Then, grimly, he lifted the small box in his hand. It weighed almost nothing. He wondered if she'd gotten him the gift before she'd decided to leave him, or after. He hoped it was after. He couldn't bear to open a gift filled with all the awful hope of her romantic dreams.

He didn't want it. He'd have to be a masochist to even look. He dropped the gift back into the tree, then went to take a shower. Taking off his wrinkled clothes, he let the scalding hot water burn down his skin. He scrubbed his hair until his scalp ached.

Perhaps it was better their marriage had ended this way. Swiftly. Cleanly. Before anyone got seriously hurt. Before they realized how little he deserved their love, when he was incapable of giving himself in return.

He remembered Holly's haunted, heartbroken face.

I love you. Can you ever love me?

And his cool, factual response as he'd told her he'd never love her. Told her it was nothing personal.

Shutting off the hot water, he stood still in the shower, remembering. His heart was pounding strangely.

Going to his walk-in closet, he tried not to look at all the designer clothes Holly had left behind, many of them still unworn, wrapped in garment bags from the boutiques. Feeling hollow, he turned away, pulling on black silk boxers and black trousers. He would call his acquisition team to tell them they needed to come in tonight. Christmas Eve be damned. Business was what mattered. Building his empire for his son to inherit—

What was in Holly's gift?

Turning on his heel, he almost ran across the bedroom to the Christmas tree. Grabbing Holly's present, he ripped off the wrapping paper and yanked open the tiny cardboard box.

Inside, tucked into white tissue paper, he saw a homemade Christmas ornament, a red felt star. He heard her sweet voice like a whisper through his heart.

My parents were happy, chasing their stars.

A lump rose in his throat. Not everyone was so lucky. Not everyone could—

"You are a fool, Stavi."

The words, spoken in Greek, were more mournful than accusing. Turning, he saw Eleni standing in the doorway.

"She chose to go. I could not stop her," he replied in the same language. The elderly Greek woman shook her head.

"She loves you. The last thing she wanted was to go."

"Her quick departure proves otherwise," he said flatly. He looked out the window at the gray morning above the gray city. He knew the stars existed above the clouds, even now. But he couldn't see them. Just like his wife and child.

He wondered if his private jet had landed yet. If the sky in Switzerland right now was bright and blue above the sparkling Alpine snow. He imagined them decorating a Christmas tree. Drinking cocoa. He saw Holly, so beautiful and loving and warm, wearing flannel pajamas tonight as she put stockings on the hearth of the old cabin's stone fireplace. She believed in love. She probably believed in Santa, too.

"Oh, Stavi." Eleni sighed, making clucking noises with her tongue. "Why did you not just tell her the truth?"

Anger went through him.

"I did," he growled. "I can never love her."

The older woman's dark eyes looked back at him, and she sighed again.

"Men," she chided, shaking her head slightly. "The truth is, you already do."

Stavros stared at her.

"Love Holly?" Ridiculous. He wouldn't love anyone. Love was a tragedy that made victims out of at least one, if not two people. He scoffed rudely, "You're out of your mind, old woman."

But she didn't let his insult stop her. "Of

course you love her. Why else would you send her away?"

"Now I know you're crazy." He looked at her incredulously. "Sending Holly away proves I love her?"

Eleni looked at him steadily. "You think you're not worthy of her. So you won't let her waste years of her life, like your mother did, loving someone who obviously doesn't deserve it."

Stavros stared at her in shock. His eyes narrowed.

"I'm nothing like my father."

The white-haired Greek woman tilted her head, her dark eyes glinting in the shadowy dawn. "No? It's true you don't sleep with other women. But do you ignore? Do you abandon and neglect?"

His hands tightened at his sides. "I've been nothing but good to them."

"You forget I've been living here lately." She lifted her chin. "While you have not."

Stavros opened his mouth to argue. Then he closed it again. Yes, all right, he hadn't been around much for the last few weeks. He'd barely seen either his new wife or his child. But he'd been trying to protect them. From loving him. Because he didn't want them hurt.

He'd tried his best. He'd given Holly his name. His money. They'd wanted for nothing.

Except his attention and love.

Because they deserved more. They deserved better.

Because he wasn't worthy.

Swallowing hard, Stavros stared out the floor-to-ceiling windows at the city.

"Go to her," Eleni said softly behind him. "If you do not, if you are not brave enough to fight for her, brave enough to give her everything, you will regret it all your life."

Silence fell.

He whirled around, but she was gone.

Pacing the room, he stopped, staring down at the red felt star his wife had made for him. He'd brought her to New York with great fanfare, promising he'd be a good husband, promising he'd be a good father, promising her she'd never regret it. Insisting he wanted to throw a party for her birthday.

Then he'd done none of it, and ghosted her.

Eleni was right. He'd abandoned his family. Not because of some business deal. And not even because he was trying to protect them.

He'd deliberately avoided his wife because he was afraid.

Afraid if she ever really got to know him, she would finally realize that she was the conqueror, not him.

My father always said loving my mother changed his life. She made him a husband. A father. More than he ever imagined he could be. He always said she changed his stars.

Slowly, Stavros held up the red felt star.

He wasn't worthy of her. That was true. He didn't know if he ever could be.

But he'd never let fear stop him before. It hadn't stopped him from building a billion-dollar company out of nothing. It hadn't stopped him from marrying Holly, though he'd somehow always known this was how it would end.

Could he change?

Could he be brave enough to give her everything?

Could he win her heart?

Tears filled his eyes as he looked out over New York City. He couldn't see the stars above the clouds, but they were there. Waiting for him to see them. Waiting to guide him.

Stavros gripped the red felt star in his hand. It was as soft as her red hair. As tender as her heart.

Blinking fast, he took a deep breath.

Maybe, just maybe…it wasn't too late to change his stars.

The Swiss valley was dark and silent, late on Christmas Eve.

Outside, the stars were bright as diamonds in the cold, black night. In the distance, Holly could hear church bells ringing for midnight mass. The road in front of her cabin was empty. Her neighbors had all gone to spend time with friends and family—those who hadn't gone to sunny climes for a holiday.

She was glad she'd taken Stavros's jet, as he'd insisted. Freddie's ears had hurt, and he'd cried the whole way. So had she. Exhausted from crying for hours, her baby had finally gone to sleep an hour before. Now, she was alone in the quiet.

Holly wondered what her husband was doing right now, back in New York. She looked out the cabin's window, but all she saw was the reflection of a young red-haired woman, lonely and sad.

No. She couldn't feel sorry for herself. She was lucky to have this cabin for herself and her child. Lucky to have time and space to figure out how to start over.

Opening the front door, Holly looked out at the quiet, wintry valley. Moonlight swept the snow, and she could see the sharp Alps high above. Her breath was white smoke dancing in the air, the icy cold a shock against her lungs. From a distance, she could see a car's lights winding down the valley road toward her tiny chalet. Someone was traveling to be with family for Christmas, she thought, and her heart felt a pang.

Shivering in her thin white T-shirt and tiny knit shorts, she closed the door, turning back inside. She had family, she told herself. Her sister had just texted her from Vermont, to tell her that the ski slopes were snowy and beautiful. Yuna's family was already stuffing Nicole with Christmas cookies and eggnog.

I think I'm going to be all right. It might take a while. But the New Year is just around the corner.

Holly smiled wistfully. Her little sister had truly grown up.

Then with a shake of her head, she started tidying up the small interior of the rustic chalet. The Christmas decorations were still up from last month. Nothing had been changed. She blessed her former employer's frantic schedule for keeping him too busy to arrange for her possessions to be packed and sent to New York.

Picking up her grandmother's old quilt from the back of the tattered sofa, Holly wrapped it around her shoulders. Taking a freshly baked sugar cookie from her chipped ceramic Santa cookie jar, she bit into it and sat down, staring at the fire.

Even the fire was different here. At Stavros's penthouse in New York, the flames had been white and without heat, fueled by cold gas, over elegant stones. Here, the fire was hot enough to warm up the cabin, fueled by split logs she kept on her porch.

When her neighbors had heard of Holly's return, they'd rushed to welcome her. Elderly Horst, bright-eyed and spry, had brought her a small Christmas tree, which he'd hewn from the nearby forest. Kindly, plump Elke had brought sugar cookies, decorated by her grandchildren.

So Holly wasn't alone. Not really. And she'd tried her best to make Freddie's first Christmas special. Her eyes lifted from the roaring fire to the two homemade knit stockings hanging over it. Before she went to bed tonight, she'd fill them with the oranges and peppermints that Gertrud had brought her, and the bag of homemade candies from Eleni. Not that Freddie could eat them yet, but at least he'd know he was loved...

The car lights outside grew brighter. Holly wondered if someone was visiting one of her neighbors. Elke's son from Germany, perhaps. Horst's brother from Geneva.

Her gaze trailed to her Christmas tree, now sparkling between the stone fireplace and the small, frosted-over window. She'd decorated it with big colorful lights and the precious vintage ornaments from her childhood. The only thing she'd left untouched in her family's old Christmas box was the garland of red felt stars. The tree seemed sparse without it. But she just couldn't.

When she'd made Stavros his homemade red felt star, she'd hoped it would start a new tradition for their marriage—blending his sophisticated Christmas tree with her own family's homespun style.

She'd only remembered her gift on the plane, when it was too late to take it back. She wondered if Stavros would even notice it, tucked amid the branches of his artificial tree, or if Eleni would toss it out with his other unwanted things.

Like Holly.

A lump rose in her throat. No, that wasn't fair. Stavros had been clear all along that he would never love her. She was the one who'd tried to change the rules. She was the one who, in spite of all his warnings, had given him her heart.

She heard the sudden slam of a car door outside, followed by the crunch of heavy footsteps in the snow. Had another neighbor decided to visit, this late on Christmas Eve? It had to be. Who else could it be—Santa Claus delivering toys for Freddie from his sleigh?

She set down the barely tasted cookie on the saucer next to her cold cocoa. Rising to her feet in her fuzzy bootie slippers, she glanced down worriedly past her mother's gold-star necklace to her old white T-shirt, so thin it was almost translucent, showing not just the outline of her breasts, but the pink of her nipples beneath. Her knit sleep shorts were so high on her thighs that they were barely better than panties. She'd dressed for solitary sobbing and brokenhearted cookie-snarfing, not to entertain guests.

A knock rattled the door, reminding her of Marley's ghost in *A Christmas Carol*. Pulling her grandmother's quilt more tightly over her shoulders, she came close to the wooden door.

Quietly, so as not to wake the tired baby sleeping in the next room, she called, "Who is it?"

For a moment, there was no answer. She wondered if she'd somehow imagined the knock, by a trick of a passing car's lights and rattle of the icy winter wind. Then she heard her husband's low, urgent voice.

"Holly..."

Now she really knew she was dreaming. She ran a trembling hand over her forehead and looked back at the sofa, half expecting to see herself still sleeping there.

"Holly, please let me in. Please."

It couldn't be Stavros, she thought. Because he never talked like that. He didn't plead for her attention. *Please* was a foreign word to him.

Frowning, she opened the door.

Stavros stood there, but a different Stavros than she'd ever seen.

Instead of his sharply tailored power suit and black Italian cashmere coat, he was dressed simply, in jeans, a puffy coat and knit beanie cap. And somehow—it didn't seem fair—his casual clothes made him more handsome than ever. He looked rugged, strong. The vulnerability in his dark eyes, shining in the moonlight, made her heart lift to her throat.

"What are you doing here?" she breathed.

"May I come in?" he asked humbly. "Please."

With a shocked nod, she stepped back, allowing him entrance to the cabin. Her knees felt so weak, she fell back against the door, closing it heavily behind her.

He slowly looked around the room, at the homespun ornaments on the Christmas tree and two stockings above the roaring fire.

"It's Christmas here," he said softly. He looked at her, and his black eyes glowed above his sharp jawline, dark with five-o'clock shadow. "The Christmas I always dreamed about."

She said hoarsely, "What do you want?"

With a tentative, boyish smile, he said almost shyly, "I want you, Holly."

Her heart twisted. Had he come all this way just to hurt her? To taunt her with what she'd never have? "You came all this way for a booty call?"

Slowly, he shook his head.

"I came to give you this." Pulling his hand out of his jacket pocket, he opened it. The red felt star she'd made him as a gift rested on his wide palm.

Looking down at it, she felt like crying. Why had he come all this way? To reject her homemade gift? To throw it callously in her face? "Do you really hate me so much?"

"Hate you?" Shaking his head ruefully, he lifted her chin gently with his hand. "Holly, you had no reason to love me. I made my position clear. I was scarred for life. I had no heart to give you. All I could offer was my name, my protection, my fortune. That should have been enough."

Holly couldn't move. She was mesmerized by his dark, molten eyes.

"But it wasn't." His lips curved at the edges. "Not for you, my beautiful, strong, fearless wife." He ran the tips of his thumbs lightly along the edges of her cheekbones and jaw. "You wanted to love me, anyway," he whispered. "Even if it cost you everything, heart and soul."

Holly shuddered beneath his touch, unable to speak.

"And now..." Stavros paused, and to her shock she saw tears sparkling in his dark eyes, illuminated by the firelight and the lights of the Christmas tree. "There's only one thing left to say."

She held her breath.

His dark gaze fell to the tiny gold necklace at her throat. Taking her hand in his larger one, he pressed something into her palm. Looking down, she saw the red felt star.

"You've changed my stars," he whispered.

She looked up. His handsome face was blurry from the tears in her eyes. She saw tears in his gaze that matched her own.

"I love you, Holly." Stavros put his hand against her cheek. "So much. And when you and Freddie left me, it was like I'd lost the sun and moon and Christmas, all at once."

She searched his gaze. "You..." Licking her lips, she said uncertainly, "You love me?"

He gave a low, rueful laugh. "I think I loved you since last Christmas Eve, when I first saw you in that red dress, standing in the candlelight of the old stone church."

With a snort, she shook her head. "You didn't act like it..."

"I hid my feelings, even from myself. I was afraid."

"You didn't want to be a conqueror," she murmured.

"I didn't want to be conquered."

"Conquered?" She choked out a laugh. "As if I could!"

He didn't laugh. "When I met you, for the first time in my life, I wanted marriage, children. I thought it was just because I wanted a legacy. Because I believed I was dying. But it wasn't."

"It wasn't?"

Stavros shook his head. "It was because of you. You made me feel things I'd never felt before. And after we slept together, I knew you could crush me if you chose." He took a deep breath. "So I pushed you away. I was afraid of hurting you. But more. I was afraid you could destroy me." Cupping her cheek, he looked down at her intently. "But I'm not afraid anymore."

"You're not?" she whispered.

"My heart is yours, Holly," Stavros said humbly. "My heart, my life, are both in your hands." His voice became low as he looked down at her hands, clasped in his own. "Can you ever love me again?"

For a moment, Holly stared at him.

Then her heart exploded, going supernova, big enough to light up the entire world. Gripping his hand, she led him to the tree and gave him the red felt star. "Put it on our tree."

With an intake of breath, Stavros searched her face. What he saw there made joy lift to his eyes. Tenderly, he placed the homemade star on a branch of the fresh-cut tree. Reaching into her family's Christmas box, she pulled out her mother's garland of red felt stars, which she wrapped beside it, around the tree.

"Now," she whispered, facing her husband with tears in her eyes, "it's really Christmas."

Love glowed from Stavros's handsome face. Then his expression suddenly changed. His dark gaze lowered to her breasts.

Holly realized that when she'd bent to get the garland, the quilt had slid off her shoulders to the floor. Her husband's eyes trailed slowly over her thin, see-through white T-shirt and the tiny knit shorts. Her body felt his gaze like a hot physical touch.

"Stavros," she breathed.

Pulling her into his arms, he kissed her, his lips hungry and hard. His jacket flew off, followed by his knit hat.

And as they sank together to the quilt on the floor, bodies entwined, Holly felt not just passion this time, but true love and commitment. The cabin was fragrant with pine and sugar cookies and a crackling fire. She'd never known joy could be like this.

And as her husband made love to her that night, on the quilt beneath the sparkling tree, Holly knew that even with the ups and downs of marriage, they'd always be happy. For there was nothing more pure than true love begun on Christmas Eve, when all the world was hushed and quiet, as two people spoke private vows, holding each other in the silent, holy night.

Three babies crying, all at once.

Stavros looked helplessly at his wife, who looked helplessly back. Then Holly's lips suddenly lifted, and they both laughed. Because what else could you do?

"I'm sorry," Eleni sighed, standing on the snowy sidewalk as she held the hand of Freddie, now fourteen months old, wailing with his chubby face pink with heat and lined with pillow marks. She continued apologetically, "I shouldn't have woken him from his nap. But I was sure he'd want to meet his new brother and sister."

Holly and Stavros looked at each other, then at their hours-old babies behind them in the third row. Stella and Nicolas had both seemed to agree, with telepathic twin powers, that they hated their car seats. They'd screamed the whole ride home from the hospital. After one particularly ear-blasting screech, Stavros had seen Colton, his longtime, normally unflappable driver, flinch beneath his uniformed cap. As if they hadn't already shocked the poor man enough by trading in the Rolls-Royce for the biggest luxury SUV on the market.

And that wasn't even the biggest change. Six months before, when they'd discovered Holly was pregnant with twins, they'd decided to move to Brooklyn, of all places.

"Our kids will need friends to play with," Holly had wheedled. "And I want to live near the other secretaries from work."

"You're friends again?"

"Most of them were finally able to forgive me for marrying a billionaire." She flashed a wicked grin. "In fact, when you're grumpy at the office, they even feel a little sorry for me..."

"Hey!"

"The point is, I don't want to raise our kids in a lonely penthouse. They need a real neighborhood to play in. Like Nicole and I had when we were young."

Eventually, Stavros had agreed. Now, he shook his head. If his father could only see him now, living in Brooklyn, surrendering to domestic bliss—and liking it! Aristides would swear Stavros wasn't his son!

His father had replaced him with a son more to his liking, anyway. After Nicole and Oliver's divorce was settled last summer, his cousin had soon found himself dumped by his wealthy lover. Facing the daunting prospect of finding a job, he'd gone to visit his Uncle Aristides in Greece, and never come back.

Now Oliver would never have to work, and Aristides had the perfect wingman to help pick up girls in bars. It was a perfect solution for them both, Stavros thought wryly.

Luckily, his wife's family wasn't as embarrassing as his own. Nicole was apparently settling in nicely to her new life in Vermont, working as a schoolteacher and dating a policeman. The relationship didn't sound serious yet, but he was sure he'd hear all the details when Nicole arrived tomorrow morning for Christmas breakfast. Whether he wanted to or not.

"Oh, dear," Eleni said, pulling him from his thoughts as she peered into the SUV's back seat with worried eyes. Freddie continued to noisily cry in harmonic counterpoint to his younger siblings. "Do you need help, Stavi?"

"May I help with the babies, Mr. Minos?" Colton offered. For Eleni to offer help wasn't unusual, but for his grizzled driver to offer to provide baby care was unprecedented. The crying must be even louder than Stavros thought.

"Yes. Thank you." In a command decision, Stavros snapped Stella's portable car seat out of the base first, then Nicolas's. He handed the first handle to Eleni, who capably slung it over one arm, and the second to his driver.

"We can manage," Holly protested beside him.

"I have someone else to worry about."

"Who could be more important than our babies?"

Stavros looked at his wife. "You."

She blushed, and protested, "I'm fine."

Fine. Stavros shook his head in wonder. Holly had spent most of yesterday, her twenty-ninth birthday, in labor at the hospital, then given birth to twins at two that morning. She should have remained in the hospital for another week, relaxing and ordering food as nurses cared for the newborns. But it was Christmas Eve, and she'd wanted to come home.

"We have to be with Freddie for Christmas, Stavros," she'd insisted. "I want to be in our new home, waking up together on Christmas morning!"

Even though mother and babies were healthy, Stavros had been doubtful they'd be allowed to leave the hospital just twelve hours after delivery. But Holly had been adamant. The instant she'd gotten her doctor's slightly bemused approval, she'd insisted on coming home.

That was his wife, he thought, shaking his head in admiration. Determined their family would be happy, and letting nothing stand in her way.

"Wait," Holly called as Eleni and Colton and Freddie started up the steps of their brownstone. "I can help—"

Now it was Stavros's turn to be adamant. "No, Holly. Be careful!"

"Wait," she cried after her children, pushing herself up from the seat before he saw her flinch and grimace with pain.

Setting his jaw, he lifted her from the SUV in his powerful arms, cradling her against his chest.

"What are you doing?" she gasped.

"Taking care of you."

"It's not necessary—"

"It is," he said firmly. "You look after everyone else. My job—" he looked down at her tenderly "—is looking after you."

And he carried her up the stoop, into their five-story brownstone.

The hardwood floors creaked, gleaming warmly as the fire crackled in the hundred-year-old fireplace. Holly had decorated the house for Christmas with her family's homemade decorations. They hadn't expected the babies to arrive early. They weren't due until January. Although when, he thought ruefully, did any Minoses let other people's expectations stand in their way?

When Holly had gone into labor yesterday, she'd stared at the three stockings on the fireplace with their embroidered names, and cried, "The twins can't be born before Christmas. I haven't made them stockings!"

Now, as Stavros carried his wife past the five stockings hanging on the fireplace, he smiled with pride when he heard her gasp.

"Nicolas... Stella—you got them Christmas stockings!" Holly looked up at him in shock. "Their names are even embroidered!"

His smile widened to a grin. "Merry Christmas, *agape mou*."

"But—" She looked at him helplessly. "How? You were with me at the hospital the whole time!"

Stavros looked down at her. "I have my ways."

"Santa? Elves?"

Lifting a dark eyebrow, he said loftily, "Call it a Christmas miracle."

She gave him a slow-rising grin. "Oh, was it now?"

"What else could it be?" He gently lowered her to her feet, then looked down at her seriously. "But not as much a miracle as this."

And putting his arms around her, he lowered his head to give his wife a tender kiss, full of love and magic, of sugarplums and sparkling stars.

After a lifetime of being frozen, it had taken a fatal diagnosis to make Stavros open his heart the tiniest crack. In that moment, Holly had gotten inside him, warming his soul with her golden light.

Once, he'd been grimly ready to die. In an unexpected miracle, he hadn't.

But Holly was the one who'd truly brought him to life.

He'd been wrong about love all along, Stavros realized in amazement. Love hadn't conquered him. It had saved him. It had set him free to live a dream greater than any he'd ever imagined. His children. His home. His wife. Especially his wife.

Being loved by Holly was the greatest Christmas miracle of all.

* * * * *

LET'S TALK

Romance

For exclusive extracts, competitions
and special offers, find us online:

f facebook.com/millsandboon

⊡ @millsandboonuk

🐦 @millsandboon

Or get in touch on 0844 844 1351*

For all the latest titles coming soon,
visit millsandboon.co.uk/nextmonth